ask Willie

the misadventures of Willie Plummet

PAUL BUCHANAN
& ROD RANDALL

CPH
SAINT LOUIS

The Misadventures of Willie Plummet

Cover illustration by John Ward.
Back cover photo by Ira Lippke.
Cover and interior design by Karol Bergdolt.

Copyright © 1999 Paul Buchanan
Published by Concordia Publishing House
3558 S. Jefferson Avenue, St. Louis, MO 63118-3968
Manufactured in the United States of America

Library of Congress Cataloging-in-Publication Data

Buchanan, Paul, 1959-
    Ask Willie / Paul Buchanan & Rod Randall.
        p. cm. — (The misadventures of Willie Plummet)
    Summary: Willie's practical jokes get him into almost as much trouble as the answers he gives in the school newspaper's advice column when he begins to rely on his own ideas rather than offering advice based of God's wisdom.
    ISBN 0-570-05478-8
    [1. Schools—Fiction.   2. Practical jokes—Fiction.] 3. Christian life—Fiction.]
    I. Randall, Rod, 1962- . II. Title. III. Series: Buchanan, Paul, 1959-   Misadventures of Willie Plummet.
    PZ7.B87717As 1999
    [Fic]—dc21

                                                98-50569
                                              AC

1   2   3   4   5   6   7   8   9   10   08   07   06   05   04   03   02   01   00   99

For Rachel and Daniel

Contents

The Oldest Practical Joke in the Book

"You hear about the game yesterday?" Felix asked me. He was sitting next to me in the crowded Glenfield Middle School cafeteria, waiting for Sam.

"What about the game?" I asked.

"Vincent Espinoza didn't get a single hit," Felix said. "He was swinging at everything. He swung at one pitch that took two bounces before it reached him."

"Nah," I said. "Impossible. Not Vincent Espinoza. Who told you that?"

"No one," Felix said. "I was *there*, Dude. I saw the whole thing. He was choking so bad I nearly ran out on the field and gave him the Heimlich."

I laughed. "Did we lose?" I asked him.

"By 12 runs is all."

"No way," I said. "We haven't lost a game all season."

"We did yesterday," Felix said. "If Vincent isn't playing well, our team stinks. He's the only one who can actually hit the ball."

"Man," I said. "Everyone thought this was the team that would get the Glenfield Gophers to state. Everyone said we'd go undefeated this season—all because of Vincent."

I looked up and saw Amy McArthur heading through the cafeteria straight for our table, carrying her tray. Felix had put his backpack on the seat across from us to save it for Sam, but Amy just picked it up, dumped it on the table, and sat down.

"You're just the guys I wanted to see," she said grinning.

"That seat was saved," Felix told her.

"No duh," she said, but she didn't move. Felix looked at me and shrugged. There was nothing we could do. Amy was a ninth grader: she outranked us. Felix sighed, took his backpack and set it on the floor beside him. He bent over his tray and started eating ravioli.

"What did you want to see *us* for?" I asked.

Amy pushed her tray out of the way and leaned in. "You guys remember last year when we took the field trip to the Pepperville Zoo?"

I remembered it well. It was the day Felix and I pulled the oldest practical joke in the book on the school bully. My stomach twisted. I could see it coming—she was going to call in a favor. I looked over at

Felix. He was too interested in his ravioli to pay attention.

"Yeah," I said. "We remember."

"Remember how you guys thought it would be funny to fill Leonard Grubb's sunscreen bottle with mayonnaise?"

I winced. This was going to be a *big* favor. "Yeah," I sighed. "I remember."

"Remember how he got a bad sunburn *and* got attacked by those big flies?"

"Yeah," I said. "Who could forget?"

"Remember how he was going to kill you and Felix because you're the two biggest practical jokers in school, and he knew you must be behind it?"

I nodded.

"Remember how *I* convinced him that it wasn't mayonnaise; it was just that his sunscreen had reached its expiration date?"

"Yeah," I said. I wished she'd get to the point.

"Well, since I saved *your* skins back then, there's something I need you two to do for *me*."

"What kind of something?" I asked. I elbowed Felix; after all he was involved in this too. He looked up from his ravioli. It was clear he had no idea what was going on. "What kind of favor are you asking Felix and me to do?" I said to help clue Felix in.

"It's nothing really," Amy said. "At any rate it's nothing compared to the danger I faced when I went to bat for you with Leonard Grubb."

"Okay," Felix said. "Whatever." He went back to eating ravioli.

Amy leaned in closer. "Here's the deal," she said. "I'm moving. Dad got a new job, and we're heading to the West Coast."

"Gee, that's a shame," I told her, hoping she'd show a little mercy. "We'll sure miss you."

"Well, I'm giving you guys something to remember me by," she said grinning.

"Really?" Felix said, suddenly alert. He swallowed the ravioli he'd been chewing. "I didn't know you were leaving. I didn't get you anything."

Amy looked at Felix a long time. She never seemed to know how to take him. "Don't get excited," Amy told him. "I'm not giving you a present. I'm giving you my job at the school paper. Friday's my last day, and Miss Pell hasn't found a replacement—I need someone to fill in for a few weeks."

Felix looked suddenly alarmed. He glanced over at me for help. I'd have to get us out of this. "Gee, Amy," I said. "We'd love to, but both of us are real busy, what with school and church and—and—" I struggled to think of what else Felix and I did that made us so busy.

Felix was thinking hard too. His eyes darted around the room. "Gymnastics," he blurted out. "We're very busy with gymnastics."

Gymnastics? I glanced up at the wall. There was a big banner for a girls' gymnastics team fund raiser. I glared at Felix.

"Yeah," I said to Amy, trying to play along. "Gymnastics takes up a lot of our time. What with jumping over that big leather thing—" I ran a finger around the inside of my T-shirt collar. "And twirling around on those other things." I made a twirling motion with my index fingers. I looked at Felix.

"And the tumbling and the rolling around," Felix put in. "And all those dismounts. Who has time?"

"We're *real* busy," I told Amy. "Maybe you can ask someone else."

Amy nodded. It was clear she wasn't buying our excuse—and who could blame her? "I understand," she said. She looked from me to Felix and back again. "You're right," she said. "You're both too busy. Maybe I *should* ask someone else."

I smiled. I couldn't believe it. She was going to let us off the hook.

"Let's see, now," Amy said tapping her chin and squinting up at the ceiling like she was deep in thought. "Who should I ask?" She snapped her fingers suddenly. Felix jumped. "I've got it," she said. "I'll ask Leonard Grubb." She grinned. "And while I'm at it, I'll fill him in on what really happened with his sunscreen that day at the zoo."

"What!?" Felix gasped.

"I can see the headline now," Amy said, spreading her hands out in the air in front of her. "School Bully Kills Two Over Harmless Prank."

"This is blackmail," I told her.

Amy thought about it a moment. "Actually, I think it's more of a straightforward threat," she said.

"You can't *do* this," Felix told her. "This isn't fair."

"Look, guys," Amy said. "A week from now I'm going to be living in California. I'll be going to a new school. I'll be trying to make new friends. I've got a lot on my mind." She sat back in her chair. "I promised Miss Pell I'd find someone to take my place on the *Gopher Gazette* for a few weeks. Like it or not, you guys are that someone. If you want out, then *you* find a replacement."

"But what do we have to do?" Felix asked. "What was your job on the paper?"

"I turned in one feature story every week, and I wrote the *Ask Amy* column." The *Ask Amy* column was an advice column where people wrote in about their problems. I hardly ever read it—it seemed like the kind of thing only girls read. There was no way I was going to write *that*.

"Okay," I said. "I wouldn't mind writing a feature story for a few weeks. It might be fun."

"No way," Felix said. "You're not sticking *me* with that lame advice column—no offense, Amy."

"None taken," Amy said. She was sitting back in her seat with her arms folded, obviously enjoying herself.

"Felix," I said, "the advice column could be a lot of fun too. You could really help people. They'd write letters about their problems, and you'd tell them what to do. You'd be great."

"No, *you* should do it," he said. "You're a natural. You're always telling *me* what to do."

"Like when!?"

"Like now!"

Amy stood and picked up her tray. "I don't care who does it, as long as it gets done," she said. "I'm out of here. Talk to Miss Pell. She'll tell you your deadlines."

Just then Sam came up to our table with her tray and looked around for an open seat. "Don't worry, Sam," Amy told her. "I was just leaving." Amy looked down at Felix and me. "Don't let me down," she warned us. "I can still *write* to Leonard Grubb from California." She walked away, carrying her tray. Sam sat down.

"What was *that* all about?" Sam wanted to know.

"Amy's moving to California," I told her. "She wants Felix and me to take over her work at the *Gopher Gazette*. We kind of owe her a favor."

"Willie's going to write the advice column," Felix chimed in.

"I advise *you* to shut up," I told him. I turned to Sam. "One of us gets to be a reporter and the other has to be *Ask Amy*," I explained. "Neither of us wants to do the advice column."

Sam looked from me to Felix and back again. "I'm not sure I'd want *either* of you giving people advice," she said.

"Are you kidding?" Felix said. "Willie would be great at it." He gave me a pat on the back. "I take his advice all the time." Felix was starting to tick me off.

"Seriously," I said to Sam. "Which one of us do you think would give the best advice?" I leaned way back in my chair and secretly nodded in Felix's direction.

Sam ignored me. "Why not just flip a coin?" she suggested. "Loser gets the advice column."

I looked at Felix. "I'm game," I said.

"Who's got a quarter?" Felix asked. I felt in my pockets, though I was pretty sure I didn't have any change. Felix didn't have any coins either. We both looked at Sam.

"You know I don't carry anything smaller than a $20 bill," she said.

"This is pathetic," I groaned. "How are we going to decide?"

"How about that rock, paper, scissors thing?" Felix suggested.

"How about a *gymnastics* tournament?" I chided. I was pretty annoyed with Felix.

"Hey, back off, Willie," Felix told me. "It was the first thing that popped into my mind. I didn't hear *you* come up with anything better."

I was really mad now. "I *would* have if you hadn't jumped in with that gymnastics thing."

"*Vaulted* in, you mean," Felix grinned. He never seemed to know when it was the right time to make a joke. I felt like pounding him.

"I think rock, paper, scissors is a good idea," Sam said.

"All right," I said, exasperated. "Best two out of three."

"One, two, three," Sam counted while Felix and I pounded our fists on the cafeteria table. I was scissors; Felix was paper. I felt instantly relieved. All the anger and frustration drained away.

"I can see it now," I said, spreading my hands out in front of me the way Amy had done. "Feedback From Felix."

"It's best two out of three," Felix reminded me. "I can still win this thing."

"One, two, three," Sam counted. Felix was paper again—but I was a rock. Suddenly I was ticked again.

"Here comes the tie-breaker," Sam announced. "One, two ..."

My mind raced. I knew Felix wouldn't be paper three times in a row, so I decided on rock. If he was scissors, I'd win. If he was a rock, we'd tie.

"Three," Sam said.

I looked down at our hands. Mine was a fist. Felix's was open, like he'd just karate-chopped the table. I couldn't believe it. "Paper!?" I said. "You did paper *three times in a row*? What are you thinking? Don't you know how to play this game?"

"I won, didn't I?"

"Yeah," I sputtered. "But nobody does the same thing three times in a row. It doesn't make any sense. You can't win if you do the same thing every time."

"Hello," Felix said. "I *did* win."

"I know," I said. "But it wasn't fair." I felt a headache coming on.

"It was fair from where I'm sitting," Sam said. I rested my forehead on my hand.

"I can see it now," Felix said. He spread *his* hands out in front of him. "Wisdom From Willie."

I groaned. "If I have to do this, I don't want anyone to know it's me giving the advice," I said. "I'll only do it if I can keep the name *Ask Amy*."

"Talk to Miss Pell," Sam suggested. "She'll probably let you keep Amy's name on the column."

Felix and I were already sitting together, so we didn't move. Even though I was still ticked at Felix, I wasn't going to pair up with anyone else. I watched as the rest of the class found partners.

Leonard Grubb just sat there near the top of the bleachers like a pile of laundry. No one went near him, and no one wanted to be the last to find a partner—because then they'd get stuck with him.

Big Ernie stood in front of me on the gym floor looking up at the bleachers, hoping to find a partner. Ernie was hard to miss: a big blonde guy with fair skin and stooped shoulders. He was taller than everyone else in the class—including Leonard—and that seemed to make him self-conscious. He was just about the shyest person in Glenfield Middle School.

Just looking at him, you'd think Ernie would be a great athlete—he was tall and muscular for an eighth grader—but he was always the last kid picked when we were choosing teams. He was too shy and uncoordinated to be any good at sports. I could tell by the look of panic in his eyes that there was no one but Leonard left without a partner.

"Ernie," Coach Askew barked. "Looks like you're with Leonard today."

Ernie swallowed hard and looked down at his feet as he climbed up next to Leonard.

Coach linked his hands behind his back and spread his feet apart, as if someone had told him to be "at ease." He eyed us coolly, his clipboard under one

Piñata boy

My last class of the day was PE. It was the only class I had with Felix. Today was Monday, so I pulled my clean gym clothes out of my backpack. I'd washed them myself on Sunday night—like I always do—so they were clean and fresh-smelling.

In a few minutes the whole PE class sat on the bleachers in the gym while Coach Askew took roll. Coach Askew was also the baseball coach, and he seemed pretty angry today—probably because the baseball team had ruined its perfect record yesterday.

Felix and I sat next to each other on the lowest bleacher. I looked behind me at the rest of the class. Leonard Grubb was sprawled out at the very top of the bleachers, all by himself. It made me a little nervous just knowing he was behind me.

"Okay," Coach Askew bellowed when he had called the last name on his clipboard. "I need you men to pair up. Each of you needs a spotter."

arm. "We'll be spending the next four weeks on the Governor's Physical Fitness Exam," he bellowed. "Each of you will be tested in 16 different areas of fitness. You'll be pushed to the limit to see which of you are good enough to join the elite ranks of the Governor's Physical Fitness Team."

"You'd think we were trying out for the Navy SEALs," Felix whispered. I grinned.

"Today's test will involve roping," Coach shouted.

"*Roping*?" Felix whispered to me. He looked suddenly nervous. "You mean like catching cows with a lasso?"

"No," I told him. "I think he means *climbing* ropes."

"Oh," Felix said, obviously relieved. "That's much easier."

Coach took us over to one corner of the gym and made us sit down. A thick rope hung down from one of the gym's steel girders. It dangled within a few inches of the gym's wooden floor. Near the top of the rope was a big plywood disk painted red.

Coach held the rope in his hand. "This is the first activity in the Governor's Physical Fitness Exam," Coach barked. "Each man simply climbs to the top of the rope and knocks on the wood so I can hear it down here. Any questions?"

Felix grinned and raised his hand. Coach pointed at him.

"I've *seen* the Governor," Felix said. "I don't think he could do this."

I groaned and held my forehead. Like I said, Felix never seemed to know when it was the right time to make a joke. Coach glared at Felix a few seconds. He wasn't in a good mood.

"All right, funny man," Coach shouted. A vein stuck out on his forehead. "You just moved to the front of the line. You're going to show everyone how it's done."

Felix swallowed. He wasn't much of an athlete, and I knew he'd never climbed a rope before. He stood up and joined Coach by the rope.

"Where's your spotter?" Coach barked. "You need your spotter."

I sighed and joined them in front of the class. Felix looked up at the red plywood circle high at the top of the rope. He looked nervous.

"You can do it," I whispered to him. "This is easy for little, skinny guys like you." Felix gave me a look. I know my words weren't very encouraging, but it was the best I could come up with right then. Felix rubbed his palms on his gym shorts and got a grip high up on the rope.

"Once he climbs higher than your head, you sit on the floor and hold the rope steady," Coach told me.

Felix swung up onto the rope and started climbing. After he'd climbed a few feet and realized how easy it would be, he got a gleam in his eye. I sat on the wooden floor and held the rope steady. I watched Felix scoot up the rope with ease. Halfway up, he started humming the theme from *Rocky*.

When he got to the top, he hummed louder and rapped out the rhythm of the tune on the wooden disk. Then he slid down the rope grinning like a jack-o-lantern. I rolled out of the way before he landed on me. He dropped to the floor like Spiderman and took a bow. Most of the guys were laughing by now, and a few gave Felix a round of applause.

"Knock it off, Patterson," Coach Askew barked, red-faced with anger. Flecks of spit flew from his mouth as he shouted. "This isn't a circus." He wasn't pleased that Felix was one step closer to joining the elite ranks of the Governor's Physical Fitness Team.

It was my turn next. I took longer than Felix did, but I made it without too much trouble and sat down on the gym floor to relax and watch the others.

Coach called on Leonard and Ernie last. Ernie came to the front of the class blushing and stooped. Coach told Leonard to go first. Leonard scooted to the top of the rope, rapped on the wood and slid back down.

It was Big Ernie's turn now—the last one in the whole class. Ernie stood on his tiptoes and got a grip on the rope. He swung his legs up onto the rope and just hung there. The class fell silent. We waited a few seconds, but Ernie just dangled there, his face beet-red. It was like he'd forgotten how to work his arms and legs.

After a few seconds he took a deep breath. He groaned with effort, trying to pull himself up the rope, but he only scooted a few inches and then stalled again.

"Come on, Ernie," I called up to him from where I sat on the gym floor. "You can do it." Ernie's feet dangled about even with Leonard's chest, and he was stuck there, twisting on the rope. It was hard to figure—Ernie was a muscular guy. He should have been able to climb that rope easily, but there he hung.

Leonard Grubb peered up at him and grinned. "Come on, you big oaf," he said. "You afraid of getting a nose bleed?"

A few of the kids snickered. It seemed impossible, but Ernie's face turned a deeper shade of red. He looked up at the red disk high above him and then down at the gym floor. He clamped his feet tighter to the rope. He wasn't going anywhere.

"Get him," Leonard said gesturing up at Ernie with his thumb. "Piñata Boy." More kids laughed this time. My stomach twisted.

"Why does he let Leonard talk to him that way?" I whispered to Felix. "He's twice as big as Leonard. He could use *Leonard* as a piñata if he wanted to."

Felix looked up at Ernie and shook his head. "He's never going to stand up to Leonard for the same reason he's never going to make it to the top of that rope," Felix said softly. "He hasn't got a shred of confidence."

Ernie still dangled there, parked four feet off the ground, utterly humiliated. I watched while Leonard untied Ernie's shoelaces and then knotted them to the rope, so he wouldn't be able to get down. Coach Askew pretended not to see. He seemed to want to take last night's baseball loss out on someone, and Ernie was the one.

"I wish Ernie'd get some confidence soon and give Leonard a pounding," I told Felix.

The bell rang, and everyone headed for the locker room, including Coach. Felix and I went over and unknotted Ernie's shoelaces. He dropped down to the gym floor. He kept his eyes on the floor as the three of us trudged back to the locker room.

"It's okay," I told him. "You'll get it next time."

Big Ernie didn't say anything. He just kept looking down at his feet as we walked through the locker room door.

I went up to Miss Pell's classroom straight from PE. I stood outside her door a few seconds trying to gather up courage. Miss Pell had a reputation as the meanest English teacher in school. She wore her hair in a tight bun and liked to peer at you over her glasses. My brother Orville insisted Miss Pell hadn't given an *A* since the Carter administration. People said she could hear every whisper in the back row. Some said she could hear dog whistles.

I was sweating when I finally turned the knob, but I told myself it was because I just came from PE. I silently pushed the door open a crack and peeked in. Miss Pell looked up from her work at her desk near the front of the room. She must have heard me breathing.

"Come in," she told me.

I took a deep breath and pushed the door open.

"Wilbur Plummet," she said. She had me in class last year, and she didn't sound too excited to see me again.

"Hi, Miss Pell," I said. I just stood there in the doorway, frozen.

"May I be of assistance?" Miss Pell asked, looking at me over her glasses.

I swallowed again. "Well, yeah," I said. One of Miss Pell's eyebrows arched suddenly. It was a reaction she had to poor grammar. "I mean *yes*." The eyebrow went back down. Just talking to Miss Pell felt like riding a unicycle.

"And *how* may I be of assistance?"

"I was told to come talk to you about taking over the *Ask Amy* column."

She tapped a pencil on her desktop. "You were sent by whom?"

"Amy was ... whom ... sent me." The eyebrow jerked upward again. I knew it sounded wrong!

Miss Pell eyed me over her glasses. "Well to be honest, Wilbur, you wouldn't have been my choice for the job," she told me. "I was hoping we'd find someone more sensitive and articulate."

"Actually, I was hoping that too," I told her. "Amy said this was just a temporary thing until you found a permanent replacement. I'm just kind of helping her out because I owe her a favor."

Miss Pell's eyebrow was up so high, it looked like it might never come down. "Very well," Miss Pell sighed. "I suppose this arrangement will suffice until a permanent alternative is located."

I just stood there. I had no idea what she'd just said.

"Is there anything else?"

"Well, yes," I said. In my head I tried to formulate a sentence that would settle Miss Pell's eyebrow back in place. "Would it be … possible … to have the title of the column … remain … unchanged … when I take over?"

The eyebrow stayed down. I heaved a sigh of relief.

"Keep calling the column *Ask Amy* until a permanent author can be located?" Miss Pell said. She pursed her lips and looked up at the ceiling, mulling it over. "I think that is advisable," she said. "You won't mind writing anonymously?"

I smiled. "Nope," I told her. The eyebrow jerked upward again. I think I jumped a little.

Et Tu, Mom?

When I left Miss Pell's classroom I had a large manila envelope tucked into my math book. Inside were the first three letters I'd be answering as the temporary *Ask Amy* writer. I had to turn my column in to Miss Pell by tomorrow afternoon, so it could be in Friday's paper.

I opened the envelope and skimmed the letters as I walked to my locker. What could I tell these kids that would help them with their problems?

At my locker I tried to think of what homework was due tomorrow. The more I thought about it, the more depressed I got—I had something due in every single class. I stuffed my backpack with books. I could barely lift it. I struggled to get both straps over my shoulders. This was not going to be a fun evening.

To top it off, I had to walk home on my own. Felix and Sam had already left. As I walked through the neighborhood streets, games of basketball had

already started up in driveways, and kids from school were riding bikes and skateboards all over the place. Was I the only kid in Glenfield who'd be doing homework all afternoon?

I passed Herbert Hoover Elementary School—the school my next door neighbor Phoebe goes to. A pickup baseball game was underway in the corner of the playground. I paused at the chain-link fence to watch a few pitches.

A kid took a big swing at a wild pitch and nearly fell over. "Who do you think you are?" another kid yelled. "Vincent Espinoza?"

Poor Vincent. A week ago he was the school hero. A week ago these kids wouldn't have dared to even *talk* to him. From hero to goat because of one bad game. Sports could be so unforgiving.

"Yo, Willie," Brad Sargent yelled from center field. "Get over here. We need more players." If I had nothing to do that afternoon, I honestly wouldn't have joined in the game. But feeling the straps of my backpack cut into my shoulders and thinking of all the work I had to do that night, I convinced myself there was nothing I'd rather be doing than playing baseball.

"Sorry, Brad," I called back to him. "Too much homework." I sighed and turned toward home. In a few minutes I was trudging up my driveway feeling very put-upon.

"Hi, Willie," a voice said. I looked over. Phoebe was sitting on her front porch next door trying to play jacks.

"Hi, Phoebe."

"Watch this," Phoebe begged. "I've been practicing. Come over here."

I groaned. "I've got tons of work to do, Phoebe," I told her. "Can't it wait till tomorrow?"

"It'll only take a second," Phoebe said. "I've been practicing all week so I could show you."

Phoebe is 9 years old. She's lived next door to me all her life, and she's had a crush on me the whole time. I'd watched her trying to play jacks for years, and I knew that no amount of practice would help. Phoebe might get straight A's, she might read on a twelfth-grade level, she might even have placed seventeenth in the state spelling bee—but she was a complete klutz.

I sighed and dragged myself over to where she sat on her front porch. "All right," I said. "Make it quick."

With me standing over her, Phoebe suddenly went stiff. Just having me there made her nervous. She cupped the tiny red ball in her hand. Her tongue appeared in the corner of her mouth. "Okay," she said. "Here goes."

She bent over the jacks. The hand with the ball moved up and down a few times, getting ready for the toss. She held her breath and tossed the ball in the air. With a jerky movement she tried to scoop up all the jacks, but she only managed to scatter them down the front steps. At the same instant, the ball ricocheted off her forehead and bounced into the bushes that bordered her driveway.

"You *have* been practicing," I told her. "I've never seen it done that way before." She was speechless with embarrassment.

At that moment something occurred to me. I guess it was because of Amy and all her talk about Leonard's sunscreen—and the fact that I'd had such a lousy day—but right then I realized that it had been a few weeks since I'd pulled my last practical joke. And it had been *months* since I'd pulled one on Phoebe. Playing pranks is like speaking a foreign language— you have to keep up with it or you get rusty.

"You should forget about jacks for now," I told Phoebe.

"I should?" she said.

"Sure," I told her. "I just passed Hoover Elementary. There's a big baseball game going on. Brad Sargent told me to send you over. He wants you to play third base."

Phoebe's eyes got large. "Brad Sargent asked for me?" she said. "I hardly know him. He's in junior high."

"Well, *he* must know *you*," I said. "He asked for you by name."

"Really?"

"Absolutely," I told her. "Better grab your glove and get over there."

Phoebe scooped up her jacks and dashed into her house, tripping on the doorway threshold.

I headed back up the front steps to my house and through the front door. I still had a ton of work to do tonight, and I'd probably have to stay up pretty late to get it all done, but the picture of poor Phoebe showing up at Herbert Hoover Elementary school with her glove, expecting to play baseball with a bunch of junior high boys cheered me up quite a bit. There's nothing like a good practical joke to brighten your day.

When I got up to my room, I dumped my heavy backpack on the bed and went to the front window. Sure enough, I saw Phoebe skipping up the street with her black baseball glove on one hand. I had to smile.

I was halfway through my write-up on Julius Caesar for my world history class when Mom called up the stairs to me. I went to my bedroom door and opened it. "I'm up here," I yelled downstairs.

"I need you to go to the store," Mom shouted up to me. "We're out of butter."

I glanced over at my desk and my open history book. "I'm kind of in the middle of something," I shouted back. "I've got a lot of homework."

"It'll only take a few minutes," she shouted. "I need you to go right away."

I puffed up my cheeks and rubbed the back of my neck. It was going to be a long night, but it would be even longer if I got Mom mad at me. "Okay," I shouted. "I'll be right down."

That night after dinner I went up to my room and got started on my homework again. By the time I was done, it was past my usual bedtime—and I still hadn't looked at the Ask Amy letters. I took the manila envelope out of my backpack. I flattened it out on my desk and looked at it a few seconds before I opened it and pulled out the letters.

There were only two letters in the envelope now. I knew there should be three because I'd read them all on the way to my locker. I looked in the envelope again. Nothing. I looked on the ground around my desk and in my backpack. Nothing. I flipped through each of my textbooks page by page. Nothing.

I groaned. I hadn't even started my first Ask Amy column, and I'd already messed up!

In my mind I retraced my steps from Miss Pell's class to this moment. The missing letter had to be in my locker. It was the only explanation. Maybe I could find it in the morning and write a response during my first period class with Mr. Keefer. I vaguely remembered what the missing letter said—something about not being popular; it wouldn't be hard to come up with some kind of answer.

I sat at my desk and read the first letter. I was so tired, I had to read it two or three times to get what it was talking about.

Dear Amy,

I'm not very good at sports and I don't like them very much. But my dad played football in college, and my mom plays tennis practically every day. They keep trying to get me to play sports, but I'm really bad and they end up getting mad at me. I'd rather be inside reading or watching TV. What should I do?

Juan Nuñez

I rubbed my eyes and pulled a pad of paper and a pencil from my desk. It was close to midnight now. I leaned back in my chair and looked up at the ceiling. Personally, I love sports, so it was hard to imagine what it would be like to hate them. But I figured if I could think of some passage in the Bible that was similar, I'd be okay.

I thought about verses our youth pastor had talked about recently. I remembered 1 Corinthians 12 about how we are all parts of the body of Christ. Each of us has gifts, but we all have *different* gifts—"If the whole body were an eye, where would the sense of hearing be? If the whole body were an ear, where would the sense of smell be?" The important thing is to find out what our gifts are, so we can use them well.

Maybe the same kind of principle applied to Juan's case. Sure, his parents were good athletes, but maybe *his* gifts lay elsewhere. I tore out a piece of paper and began writing.

Dear Juan,

What you've got to remember is that your parents want you to have a better life than theirs. (Maybe your dad wishes he could have played professional football after college. Maybe your mom wishes she could have made it to Wimbledon.) Your parents want you to be better than them at the things they're good at. They'll feel better once they realize you're good at other things.

Usually when parents make your life difficult, it's only because they want you to be healthy, happy, and successful-even more than they are. Try to show them you can be healthy, happy, and successful without being good at sports. Find something you do well, and show them how good you are at it. All they really want to know is that you'll be okay in the future when they can no longer help you.

Amy

I read my answer over. I was too tired to know if it was making any sense. It wasn't *exactly* like in 1 Corinthians, but I thought it was probably pretty good advice.

I yawned and read the second letter.

Dear Amy,

My little brother is driving me crazy. He's always getting me in trouble. Mom and Dad always take his side and I get punished. He gets everything he wants and I just get ignored. I used to lick him, but now I don't. What should I do?

Steven Singleton

I smiled. If I didn't know better, this letter could have been written by Orville. My whole life he's been telling me I get all the breaks. He doesn't notice all the things *he* gets as the older brother.

I guess sibling rivalry is nothing new. The Bible is full of jealous brothers—starting with the first two brothers in history. I thought about Philippians 4 where it tells us to be content in all things. I wondered how I could explain the apostle Paul's principle to Steven. I rubbed my eyes and started writing on a fresh sheet of paper.

Dear Steven,

Little brothers are supposed to drive their older siblings crazy. It's part of their job.

Your parents love both of you—they probably just have different ways of showing it. I know it sometimes seems like your little brother has it easy, but as the older brother you get a lot of privileges your younger brother doesn't—maybe

you get to stay up later or you get to go hang
out at the mall with your friends. Just try to be
content and to notice all you have to be thankful
for.

Maybe your parents aren't ignoring you.
Maybe they're just trusting you and giving you
the freedom and responsibility your little brother
isn't ready for.

By the way, I'm glad to hear you no longer
lick your brother. That can't be much fun for
either of you.

Amy

I read the letter over and grinned at the last paragraph. Miss Pell would probably cut it out, but I
couldn't resist.

When I was done proofreading my answers, I
stuffed everything back into the manila envelope and
went in the bathroom to brush my teeth. I stared in
the mirror. My eyes were glassy and drooping. I spat
the toothpaste into the sink, rinsed it down, and
trudged back to my bedroom.

I dragged myself over to bed and pulled my paja-
mas on. I pulled down my covers and rolled between
the cold sheets. I was so tired, it took a few seconds
for me to realize what was wrong: my knees were up
under my chin. I tried to push my legs down to the
end of the bed, but there was no way. Someone had
short-sheeted my bed!

I groaned. It had to be Orville. I couldn't believe he would stoop to such an infantile practical joke— short-sheeting went out with sixth-grade camp. If mayonnaise in the sunscreen bottle was the oldest practical joke in the book, short-sheeting a bed must have been in the table of contents.

Any other night I would have just laughed and started planning my revenge. But tonight I was so exhausted, it really got me mad. I rolled out of bed and angrily stripped off all the blankets and sheets. Yawning and cold, I started remaking my bed.

"You hit a new low, Orville," I told him when I came down to breakfast the next morning. I'd had trouble waking up, so I was late for breakfast. Dad and Amanda had already left. Orville sat at the table alone, eating cereal and reading the box. An empty milk container sat at his elbow. He was humming to himself as he chewed.

"Why not just stick a sign on my back that says, 'I have cooties?'" I asked him.

"What are you talking about?" Orville said. He put down the cereal box and looked up at me.

"Short-sheeting my bed," I said. "Couldn't you come up with something more original?"

"I don't know what you're talking about," Orville said. "I didn't go anywhere near your bed." He picked up the cereal box and started reading again.

"I hate to interrupt while you're studying for your Lucky Charms final," I said, pulling out a chair. "But who else would have done it?"

"Phoebe," my mom said. She came through the swinging kitchen door with a new jug of milk.

"Huh?"

"Phoebe was the one who short-sheeted your bed," Mom informed me.

"How do you know that?"

"I helped her."

"What!?" I said.

"She came over here yesterday and told me about the mean trick you played on her," Mom told me. "She asked if she could short-sheet your bed. I thought it was a wonderful idea, so I sent you to the store for butter."

My mind was reeling. My own mother had betrayed me. "You were in on it?" I sputtered. "You let Phoebe in my room?"

"We tried to do it from the doorway, Dear, but our arms weren't long enough." Everyone in my family is a comedian. Mom put the new jug of milk on the table and picked up the empty one.

"I can't believe you helped Phoebe short-sheet my bed," I said. I collapsed into my chair at the table. "Stabbed in the back by my own mother."

"You had it coming, Willie," she told me. "Now eat your breakfast." She disappeared through the swinging door into the kitchen.

④

The Great Parking Lot Conspiracy

The minute I stepped out the door I could hear Phoebe giggling. I looked around for her. She was peeking around the edge of her garage.

"Very funny," I told her. "But as a practical joke, that one was purely amateur. At least you haven't ruined your Olympic status."

"I thought it was pretty good," Phoebe said, grinning.

"Good for a fifth grader," I told her. "But it's nothing compared to the devious one I'm going to play on you in the near future." The smile faded from her face. "You'll never see it coming," I told her. "Be afraid. Be *very* afraid." Phoebe looked genuinely concerned now. I grinned and headed down the driveway toward school.

As soon as I opened my messy locker, I remembered the missing letter. It had to be in here somewhere; it couldn't just disappear. If I found it, I could still put together some kind of answer during Mr. Keefer's class. I started taking everything out of my locker and putting it on the ground.

"What are you doing?" Sam asked me. I jumped. She had a way of sneaking up behind me. Sam peeked over my shoulder into my nearly empty locker.

"Nothing," I said, a little ticked. "I'm just looking for something."

"What?"

"One of the letters Miss Pell gave me to answer for the *Ask Amy* column," I told her. I pulled out a couple of library books and some crumpled papers. My locker was now completely empty. The missing letter wasn't there. I sighed. "Some kid wrote a letter about how everyone ignores him and no one even remembers his name," I told Sam.

"How sad," Sam said. "Who wrote it?"

"I don't know," I told her, stuffing the library books back in my locker. "Bob, Steve—something like that. I don't remember." I crammed a few more books into my locker.

"So what are you going to do?" Sam asked.

I shrugged. "I guess I'll just have to ignore it," I told her.

Sam was silent a few seconds. I crammed the last books in my locker and slammed it shut. When I turned around, Sam was giving me one of her looks. "The *Ask Amy* column is in good hands," she told me.

I wasn't expecting a complement. I smiled. "Thanks," I told her. "Thank you very much." It was good to hear some encouraging words.

Sam didn't smile back. She just sighed and shook her head. Sometimes I had no idea what that girl was thinking.

"Willie," Felix said. "You're just the man I wanted to see. I'm glad I caught you."

"We eat lunch together every day of the week," I told him. "You didn't have to do much catching." Felix put his tray down on the table and took a seat.

"I just finished my first feature article," he told me. "I've got to turn it in to Miss Pell, and I'm kind of nervous."

"Tell me about it," I said. "I've got my *Ask Amy* column in my locker. I'll bet she sprains her eyebrow by the time she gets done with it."

"I know the feeling," Felix said. "Will you read mine over and tell me what you think?"

I put down my fork. "Sure," I told him.

Felix unzipped his backpack. "It's a really hard-hitting investigative piece," he told me. "I step on a lot of toes, but that's what a good journalist is supposed to do. I'm just hoping it doesn't get me in any hot water."

"Really?" I said. "Wow. You're taking this stuff seriously."

Felix slid his article across the table to me. It was computer printed on two pages and stapled in the corner. I thought about my column—hand written on notebook paper, slapped together in a few sleepy minutes. It was going to look pretty pathetic alongside Felix's.

School Board Places Faculty In Peril
by Felix Patterson

Mr. Lumpkin, Glenfield Middle School's custodial supervisor, reported that there has been a recent dramatic upswing in the number of car doors dented in the school's faculty parking lot. So far this year, four car doors have been dented or scratched at GMS. Only two cars were dented during the entire school year last year.

Over the summer, the parking lot was repaved and the stripes were all repainted. Mr. Lumpkin asserts that the newly painted spaces are several inches smaller than the ones they replaced. He suggests that the narrower spaces might have been used in order to make room for two extra spaces. The burning question is: are the two extra spaces worth the approximately $160 worth of damage to faculty car doors?

An investigation of Central Middle School's faculty parking lot, which has not been repaved in several years, showed that parking spaces there are four inches wider than the ones here at GMS.

In its headlong pursuit of extra parking spaces, has the school district decided that parking capacity is more important than the safety and well-being of its faculty? Did school authorities turn a blind eye to the possible consequences of this controversial move?

Members of the school board refused to return this reporter's phone calls, and Principal Abernathy was not available for comment because he was allegedly getting the oil changed in his own car (which has not yet been dented). It is this reporter's opinion that a full-fledged investigation into this important matter should be launched immediately.

When I was done reading, I made the mistake of looking up.

"What do you think?" Felix asked immediately. "Is it too hard-hitting? You think I can get away with it?"

I didn't know what to say. It was about the lamest excuse for a news story I'd ever seen. I stared down at the paper, trying to think of something to say.

"Well," I said. "It's certainly thorough ... and ... and ..." I glanced around the cafeteria as though someone might be holding up a cue card telling me what to say. To my relief, I saw Sam coming toward us with her tray.

"Here's the person you should ask," I told Felix. "Sam's the best writer in this group."

Sam sat down across from me with a suspicious look on her face. "What going on here?" she wanted to know. "I get the distinct feeling I'm being set up for something."

"Nonsense," I said. "Felix is just looking for some feedback on his first feature article." I passed the paper across the table to her.

Sam flattened it out on the table top and bowed her head in grace. "School Board Places Faculty In Peril," she read aloud when she opened her eyes again. "Sounds impressive." She picked up the squeeze bottle of ketchup in the middle of the table and squirted some on her hamburger. She took a bite and started reading.

Felix and I watched her closely while she read. Felix was smiling, bright-eyed and expectant. Sam turned the page and finished the article. She looked up at me and Felix, still chewing her hamburger. She swallowed. "You're serious?" she asked Felix. His smile disappeared.

"Of course I'm serious," Felix said. "What do you mean, am I serious?"

"I've never *been* so bored," Sam said. "And *I've* been to Smurfs on Ice."

Felix was flabbergasted. "*Bored*?" he said. "How can you say this is boring? You wouldn't know top-notch investigative reporting if it did hand-springs across the cafeteria and bit you on the nose."

"I could use a good bite on the nose to wake me up after reading this," Sam said, pushing the paper across the table to Felix.

"You don't know what you're talking about," Felix sputtered. "This story's got everything: suspense, danger, political intrigue. I'm really on to something here."

"You're talking about a *parking lot*," Sam reminded him, leaning across the table. "There's nothing interesting about a parking lot."

"It's not *just* about a parking lot," Felix nearly shouted. "It's about a whole lot more."

"What?" Sam wanted to know. "Do you think you've uncovered some vast conspiracy between Glenfield's auto body shops and its parking lot line-painters?"

"Remember," I said gravely. "The school board is in on it too. Come to think of it, it probably goes all the way to the governor's office." Felix glared at me. "Keep this up and you'll never get on his Physical Fitness Team."

"You guys don't know what you're talking about," Felix sniffed. "You'll see. Miss Pell will love this story."

"Okay," Sam said. "Whatever."

Just then I noticed a little kid standing behind Sam. At first I thought he was an elementary school kid who'd wandered onto the wrong campus, but when I looked at him again, I realized he was just the smallest junior higher I'd ever seen. Felix was pretty small, but they looked about the same height now— and Felix was sitting down!

Sam and Felix were still bickering, but the kid just stood there, as if he didn't want to interrupt.

"Can I help you?" I asked him. Sam stopped talking and looked over her shoulder at him. He immediately looked down at his shoes.

"Sorry to interrupt," he said formally. "But may I please borrow your ketchup bottle?"

Sam glanced over at me and then picked up the red squeeze bottle from the middle of our table. "Here you go," Sam said.

The kid grabbed the ketchup bottle and beat a hasty retreat. I watched him scamper over to the next table. When he sat down, he completely disappeared.

"Suddenly I feel so tall," Felix said grinning.

"Don't be mean," Sam scolded him.

When I went up to Miss Pell's room after lunch, I took Felix's article with me. He insisted that Miss Pell would love it but he was too scared of her to turn it in himself. Maybe he thought she was part of the Great Parking Lot Conspiracy.

I knocked on her door. She told me to come in. She was bent over her desk grading essays with a red felt pen. She didn't look up until I was right in front of her desk.

"Wilbur," she said. "I was afraid you weren't going to make your deadline."

"I've got my column," I told her. "I've got it right here." I set the manila envelope on her desk. "Felix's story is in here too."

"Splendid," she said. "Let's have a look."

I swallowed. "You don't got to do it right now," I told her. On the word *got*, her eyebrow launched half way up her forehead.

She pulled the papers from the manila envelope. I thought about how sleepy I was when I wrote my column. Who knows how many mistakes I made—her eyebrow might actually leap from her face. It was something I definitely didn't want to witness. "I really should be going," I mumbled.

"Just wait right here, Wilbur," she told me. "This will only take a moment."

Her eyes darted back and forth across the page. I didn't want to, but I found myself staring at her eyebrow. I was mesmerized. It was like watching someone defuse a bomb—you never knew when it might go off. I held my breath. She looked up at me suddenly over her glasses. I jumped a little.

"Well?" I asked. My mouth was dry.

"You only made one mistake," she told me. Had I missed an eyebrow jump?

"What mistake was that?"

"You're not supposed to use the writer's real name," she told me. "We always print the letters with a false name attached."

"Really?" I said. "That's the *only* thing I did wrong?"

"You sound surprised," Miss Pell said. "I think you did a fine job."

When I left Miss Pell's classroom, with a new manila envelope under my arm, I felt like doing a tap dance.

"She said I did a fine job," I told Felix that afternoon. We were in Coach Askew's PE class, sitting at the edge of the long-jump pit. This was phase two of the Governor's Physical Fitness Test. Coach Askew was glum and quiet today; his baseball team had lost its second straight game.

"I couldn't believe it," I said to Felix, still feeling giddy. "Miss Pell actually liked what I wrote!"

Dan Andrews ran down the long-jump runway and launched himself through the air into the sand pit. It was a good jump. Coach Askew measured the jump and marked it on his clipboard. Then Leonard Grubb raked the sand to cover up the footprints.

"What did she think of *my* story?" Felix wanted to know.

"I don't know," I told him. "She didn't read it while I was there."

"Well if she liked yours, she's got to *love* mine," Felix reasoned.

"Yeah, sure," I said. "I hear she's a big fan of parking lots."

"Ernie," Coach barked. "You're up."

Big Ernie stood up and trudged toward the far end of the long-jump runway. He stood there looking toward the sand pit and all the kids sitting around it. His face was beet-red again.

"Any time you're ready," Coach said without looking up from his clipboard.

Big Ernie began jogging down the runway, then accelerated to a clumsy gallop. As he pounded his way toward the long-jump pit, I saw what was about to happen. While Coach still looked down at his clipboard, Leonard Grubb squatted down next to the runway with the rake.

"Ernie," I called. "Watch—" Just as Ernie launched himself into the air, Leonard slid the rake handle in front of Ernie's feet. Ernie tripped and flew sprawling, face first into the sand pit.

Coach looked up from his clipboard. "Not much of a jump there, Ernie," he said. He jotted something down on his clipboard.

Ernie rose to his feet, dazed. His front was covered with sand. Felix and I were the only ones who weren't laughing. Ernie's chin had a smear of blood

on it. He spat out some sand and then looked back at
Leonard. He didn't say anything to Coach, he just
dusted himself off and stepped out of the pit. It
looked like he was trying to keep from crying.

"Rake it," Coach said looking down at his clipboard. Leonard began raking the sand again.

"Norris," Coach barked. "You're up next."

I looked over my shoulder to where Big Ernie sat
apart from the class, dabbing his chin with the hem of
his gym shirt.

"I wish he'd get some confidence," I said to Felix.
"I wish he'd give that Leonard a pounding."

"Yeah," Felix snorted. "And *I* wish pigs could fly."

I looked at Felix. "Really?" I said. "Have you tried
flapping your arms?"

Felix grinned and slugged me on the shoulder.

That Friday I couldn't wait to read the *Gopher
Gazette*. I'd never had anything I'd written appear in
print before. I kind of wished my name was on the
column now instead of Amy's.

I picked up a copy of the *Gazette* from the big table
outside the cafeteria where they get stacked every Friday. I held it under my arm while I went through the
cafeteria line. I had butterflies in my stomach.

I sat down at an empty table and opened the paper to my column. It was weird to see the words I'd scribbled out in pencil all neatly typeset and printed. It actually gave me goose bumps.

I looked around at all the people in the cafeteria reading the paper. It was cool to think that none of them knew I was the one who wrote this week's *Ask Amy* column.

"I can't believe it," Felix sputtered, plopping down on the seat next to me. I'd been gloating so much, I didn't even see him coming. "Did you look at my article?" Felix asked.

I'd been so busy admiring my own column that I hadn't even bothered to look for Felix's story. "No," I said. "I didn't see it." I closed my paper and looked at the front page. "Baseball Team Loses Fourth Straight Game," the headline read.

"It's not on the front page," Felix said. "It's all the way on the back."

I flipped the paper over. The back page was covered with odds and ends—the last paragraphs of a lot of stories, a cartoon, and an ad for a frozen yogurt shop. Then I noticed it. Down on the bottom right corner was a tiny headline: Parking Spaces Narrowed. Beneath the headline was one small paragraph:

> Over the summer, the parking lot was repaved and the stripes repainted. Narrower spaces might have been used to make room for

extra parking. So far this year, four car doors have
been dented or scratched at GMS.

"Wow," I said. "They really cut a lot out of your
story."

Felix nodded and glanced around. "It was too
hard-hitting," he said. He leaned closer to me. "I think
the School Board got to Miss Pell," he whispered.

I thought maybe he was joking, but when I looked
at him I saw he wasn't. "Maybe they just cut it
because there wasn't enough room," I suggested.

Felix laughed. "Yeah, right," he said. "Don't be
naive, Willie. They want to silence me. But I'm not
playing their game."

"You know, you're beginning to sound a bit paranoid," I told him. "I'm sure they were just trying to
make space."

Felix didn't seem to be listening. "No one's going
to silence Felix Patterson," he said, pushing his glasses up higher on his nose. "I'm working on a story now
that will blow the lid off a certain cafeteria condiment
scandal."

"*Condiments*?" I said. "You mean like ketchup
and mustard?"

"Shhhh," Felix hissed. He glanced around us, like
he was afraid someone might have overheard. "Mum's
the word," he cautioned me. "The investigation is cur-
rently underway."

I Come Up in the World

The next Wednesday at lunch, I was waiting at a table in the cafeteria for Felix and Sam as usual. While I waited I looked over my handwritten *Ask Amy* column. It was a lot easier to write this time—I suppose I was feeling more confident. But I still wanted to proofread it one last time before I turned it in to Miss Pell.

Dear Amy,

I have a biology teacher with a parrot named Ernie who tells the same joke over and over. (The teacher tells the joke, not the parrot--whose name is Ernie.) Every day he (the teacher) goes up to the cage and says, "How come you never talk to me anymore?" Then he laughs real loud (the teacher, not Ernie, who is the parrot). How do I get him to stop?

A Concerned Student

Dear Concerned,

Everyone has annoying quirks. I guess it's just part of being human. (I have a brother who hums when he eats and a sister who talks like a baby when she's on the phone with her boyfriend.) If you or I were to ask our friends what annoying quirks we have, I'm sure they could name a few.

I think the Golden Rule applies here: If you'd like your friends to overlook your quirks, you should be willing to overlook the quirks you see in others. With regard to the teacher and the parrot: If he (the parrot) can stand hearing the same joke every day, maybe you can too.

Amy

Dear Amy,

My mom and dad got divorced two years ago. They keep fighting and they keep trying to get me to take sides, but I don't want to.

When I'm with my dad, he always insults my mom. And when I'm home with Mom, she does the same thing. If Mom buys me new shoes, Dad buys me something even more expensive. It's like they're competing for my attention and love.

I love them both. I just want them to stop trying to get me involved in their fights. What can I do?

Torn Between Two Parents

Dear Torn,

I know it's hard to believe, but being a parent can be very scary.

When you're a baby, your parents worry that you'll get sick. When you're a kid, your parents worry that you'll get hurt falling off the monkey bars. When you're a teenager, they worry that you'll stop loving them. Let's face it: we see a lot of teenagers who treat their parents like they don't love them anymore.

Try telling your parents that you'll never stop loving them. Tell them that you love them both so much, you can't take sides. Tell them that you don't want to hear them insult each other because you love them. I think they'll get the message.

Amy

"How's it going, Amy?" a voice said. I looked up from my papers. Felix set his tray down across from me and sat down.

"Keep it down," I told him, glancing around to make sure no one had heard him. "Nobody is supposed to know I'm the one writing the column. I'd never live it down."

"Chill," Felix told me. He shrugged off his backpack and put it on the floor beside him. "My lips are sealed." He made a show of locking his lips and throwing away the key.

"Okay," I said. "But if anyone finds out, I'll know who to kill." Threats usually worked pretty well with Felix.

"Is that this week's column?" Felix nodded at the papers on the table in front of me.

"Yeah," I told him. I stuffed the papers back in the manila envelope, so no one walking by would see them. "Just keep your mouth shut."

Felix glanced around and then leaned in to talk confidentially. "Would you be disappointed if your column didn't make it in the paper this week?" he asked.

"Not really," I said. "Well, maybe a little. Why?"

"Because I finished writing the feature I told you about," he whispered. "It's a hot one. Miss Pell will probably bump your column to make room for it."

"What feature?" I asked.

"Shhh," Felix hissed. He glanced around again. "You know. The Condiment Scandal."

"Yeah, sure," I said. "The Condiment Scandal. How could I forget?"

Felix pulled his backpack up into his lap and unzipped it. He sneaked out a couple of sheets of paper and slid them across the table to me.

I sighed and started to read.

Counterfeit Condiments
by Felix Patterson

We've all seem them. Many of us have used them. We can find them any day at lunch in the cafeteria between the salt and pepper shakers. They're the plastic squeeze bottles that hold the ketchup we all use. Each bottle has the word *Heinz* printed on it in raised letters. But are we getting what we think we're getting?

Acting on a tip from a disgruntled cafeteria worker, this reporter checked the trash bins behind the kitchen, only to find two large empty ketchup cans. Rather than being cans of the best-selling, high-quality Heinz brand, these were cans of the much cheaper Sauceko brand. Is there a condiment deception afoot?

A source close to the cafeteria kitchen confirmed that cafeteria employees routinely fill the Heinz containers with inferior, discount brands of ketchup. District dietitian Rhodora Muncal claims that there is little nutritional difference between the two brands and that budgetary considerations have led to the use of discount ketchup. "It just isn't that big a deal," she claimed. "It's just ketchup."

While the substitution of discount ketchup for name-brand ketchup may pose no immediate danger, this reporter wonders where it will all end. If such condiment cut-backs continue, are we not all placed in immediate danger? What if, for example, the mayonnaise is not properly refrigerated in an attempt to save money? What effects would we all face then?

When I finished reading, I looked at the ketchup bottle in front of me and then at Felix. I didn't know what to say.

"What do you think?" Felix asked. He reached across and took the paper from me. He set it face down on the table, as if he didn't want anyone to see it.

"I don't know," I told him, trying to find the right words. "It just seems a bit …"

"Risky?" Felix said. "Hard-hitting? That's what I thought too. But *someone's* got to tell this story." Felix fell silent. He was looking at someone over my shoulder.

I turned around to see who was there. It was that very small kid—the one who borrowed our ketchup last week.

"Excuse me," he said. "I'm sorry to interrupt. But may I see your ketchup bottle?"

Felix's eyes narrowed. He stood up and leaned across the table toward the kid. "*Why*?" Felix asked. "What have you heard about the ketchup?"

The kid's eyes darted around the room. This clearly wasn't the kind of response he'd been expecting. He backed away a few steps.

"*Who sent you*?" Felix demanded.

The kid took off running. Felix sat back down again. "See that?" he said. "Word is already out."

I sighed and shook my head. "You really *have* lost your mind," I told him.

When I got to PE class I had already turned in my column to Miss Pell and she had given me a new envelope of letters. I'd have a lot more time to work on answering them this time. I locked the envelope in my gym locker with my street clothes.

I sat down on the bench that ran between the rows of lockers and tied my gym shoes. Someone from the class before had forgotten to lock their gym locker. The combination lock was hooked through the latch, but whoever put it there forgot to close the lock and spin the dial. It was just hanging open. I thought I'd do him a favor and lock it.

I pulled my shoelace tight and got up. When I bent down to click the lock shut, someone pushed me aside. I stumbled back and sat on the bench again. Leonard Grubb reached down and unhooked the open lock.

"Hey, that's not yours," I told him.

"It is now," he said.

"Come on, Leonard," I said. "What possible use is it to you? You don't even know the combination."

"Just keep your mouth shut, Plummet," Leonard growled. "I can *definitely* use it." He headed down to the end of the row of lockers, holding the stolen lock. I guessed what he had in mind.

"Come on, Leonard," I called after him. "Leave Ernie alone."

Leonard disappeared around the corner. I got up and followed him.

I turned the corner and glanced down the next row of lockers. There were a couple of kids on the bench talking, but when they saw Leonard coming, they got up, filed past me, and headed out to the playground.

The only one left in the aisle now was Big Ernie, and he was pulling his gym shirt over his head. He didn't see Leonard coming. When he pulled his shirt down, he saw Leonard and took a step backwards. It gave Leonard just enough room.

Leonard stepped in front of Ernie's locker. "Ernie, buddy," he said. "It isn't safe to leave your locker wide open like this. Someone might steal those wonderful clothes of yours." Leonard slammed Ernie's locker and hooked the stolen lock into the latch. "Let me help you."

Leonard clicked the lock shut and spun the dial. He turned to face Ernie. Ernie was red-faced again. Leonard grinned. "Don't mention it," he told Ernie. "It was my pleasure." Leonard was still grinning when he passed me and headed outside.

I looked down the row of lockers at Ernie. He sighed. He and I were the only ones in the locker room now. Coach Askew was probably taking roll, so both of us would get marked tardy—but that didn't seem important.

Ernie took hold of the lock and gave it a tug, but of course it was hopeless. He'd never get his clothes out before school let out. He'd probably have to walk home in his gym suit.

"Maybe Coach would let you call your mom," I suggested. "Maybe she could bring you some more clothes before the end of the period."

Ernie didn't answer. He just looked down at the damp locker room floor.

I didn't have much homework that night, so I started working on my column right after dinner—that way I'd be way ahead of the game. I unclasped the manila envelope and pulled out the letters. I read the top one.

Dear Amy,

There's this guy I like. I'll call him Person A. Anyway, my so-called best friend (Person B) knows this other girl (Person C), who sits next to A in social studies. Anyway, I asked B to ask C if she could tell A that I like him a lot. But instead C told A that it was B who liked him, and not me.

Now my other best friend (D) tells me that B really liked A all along and told C to tell that to A, because she knew I liked A and that I was going to get C to tell him that. D says I should never talk to B again. What do you think?

Katharine Diosan

I had to read the letter a few times before I could figure out what it was talking about. It was like one of those horrible word problems in algebra about train A leaving St. Louis heading south, while train B left Los Angeles heading west at two-thirds the speed of train A.

Dear Alphabet Soup,

I think you're making your life too complicated. There are certain things we're supposed to worry about in life—being honest, treating other people well, doing the best we can. But life can get too complicated when we start worrying about all the things we don't need to worry about. I'm convinced that if you focus on the things you're supposed to worry about, the other things will take care of themselves.

Amy

Not bad, I thought. I've only been at it 10 minutes and I've already got the first one done. I turned to the second letter.

Dear Amy,

I just got a new skateboard for my birthday. I've always wanted to learn how to ride one, but my mom says I have to wear a helmet. Only professional skateboarders wear helmets, so it makes me look like a poser. To top it off, it's big and red, and I look like a dork.

What should I do?

William Ryan

Piece of cake, I thought. This one wouldn't take long. I even had a good name for the guy.

Dear Helmet Hater,

Parents are weird that way. For some reason, they hate the idea of having their kids mangle themselves. When it comes to safety, it's hard to change a mother's mind.

The best thing you can do is wear your helmet, practice hard, and become the best skater you can be. Who knows—maybe when your mom sees how responsible you are with your skateboard, she'll change her mind about the helmet. If not, you'll soon be a good enough skater that everyone will know you're not a poser.

Amy

Two down. One to go. I turned to the third letter.

Dear Amy,

I'm on the baseball team. I'm in a hitting
slump, and it's driving me crazy. I couldn't even
get a hit playing tee-ball these days. Every
time I get to the plate, I get nervous and
tighten up. It never used to be like this. I used
to enjoy going up to bat, now I have nightmares
about it. If we lose any more games, we won't go
to the playoffs.

                         Vincent Espinoza

I couldn't believe it: the great Vincent Espinoza
was asking *me* for advice. Vincent was one of the
most popular kids in school and probably the best
athlete Glenfield had ever seen. Until he hit his batting slump, I wouldn't even have dared smile at him in
the hallway—and now he was asking me for advice.

I'll admit it. I could feel my head swelling. When I
first began to write *Ask Amy*, I just tried to think of
good advice to give people—mostly principles from
the Bible. But at that moment my perspective started
to change.

It almost felt like the fate of Glenfield's baseball
team was in my hands—and, along with it, the
school's self-esteem. I felt important. Vincent
Espinoza was a big shot. If he was coming to me for
advice, what did that make *me*?

I got out a new sheet of paper and started to
write.

Dear Vincent,

Glenfield has never made it to the playoffs,
and you're the best baseball player we've had
here in a long time. We've put a lot of pressure on
you. It must be hard to take. Not many people
work well under pressure.

What I want you to remember, though, is that
baseball is just a game. And it's a game you love.

When you go up to the plate, I want you to
take a moment to relax. Look out at the outfield
fence and imagine the ball sailing over it—the
way it's done hundreds of times before. Remember
that feeling. Remember just how much fun this
game can be.

Amy

I read the letter over. It seemed like pretty good
advice and if it managed to pull Vincent out of his batting slump, I'd be a school hero—even if no one knew
it was me.

I got up from my chair and stretched. I was feeling good. I'd come up in the world. I was now advisor
to the stars.

I was on my way downstairs to watch some television when I remembered another project that needed my attention. I went back up to my room and sat
back down at my desk. I got out a new sheet of paper
and a black pen. I started writing a letter of my own.

"Dear Dr. Griffith," I wrote neatly at the top. I grinned. This would be sweet.

Dear Dr. Griffith,

You're probably wondering why I bothered to write this letter when I'm standing right in front of you, but I have a problem and it's kind of embarrassing to talk about.

You see, I've been hearing these voices inside my head for the last year or so, and I keep seeing small animals that no one else seems to notice. But the last straw is that lately I've developed a terrible fear of lawnmowers and many other gardening tools. I can't even walk through the Home Warehouse without screaming.

Boris (the little man who lives in my sock drawer) assures me that all of this is normal and I shouldn't worry about it. But I thought I'd better come to you for a second opinion.

I read it over and then slipped it into the manila envelope Miss Pell had given me. I sealed it shut. On the front of the envelope I wrote: *Dr. Doris Griffith—Urgent and Confidential.*

I went over to my alarm clock and set if for a half hour earlier than usual.

The Governor's Ballet Troupe

The next morning I watched from my bedroom window until I saw Phoebe come down the driveway and head off for school. I ran down the stairs and out the front door. When I got to the end of my driveway, Phoebe was half way down the block.

"On your way to school?" I called after her.

Phoebe stopped and turned around. She smiled when she saw it was me. "No, Dummy," she said. "I'm on my way to the opera. What do you think?"

"Wait up," I said. "I'll walk with you."

Phoebe stood waiting for me to catch up. "Willie Plummet wants to walk with *me*?" she said. "I smell a practical joke."

"Hey," I said, holding my hands up in a gesture of innocence. "If you think I'm trying to pull something, I can just walk to school on my own." I pushed ahead of her and headed down the street.

"No, Willie," she said. "Wait up. I trust you." She jogged to catch up with me.

We walked a few seconds in silence. We turned down Carver Street. Phoebe seemed anxious to start a conversation.

"Did you hear about the game last night?" Phoebe asked. "The Gophers lost again. Vincent Espinoza hasn't had a hit in seven games now. Two more losses and you guys are eliminated from the playoffs."

I stopped in my tracks and gave her a funny look.

"*What*?" she said.

"I'm just surprised you know about our baseball team," I said. "What you don't know about sports would fill a book."

Phoebe made a face and put her hands on her hips. "What you don't know about *me* would fill a *library*," she told me.

"Whatever," I said. We started walking again. "Between you and me, I've got a good feeling about Vincent Espinoza," I told her. "I think he's going to break out of his slump real soon."

"Hey, what's this?" Phoebe said.

A manila envelope lay in the middle of the sidewalk. Phoebe picked it up and turned it over. *Dr. Doris Griffith—Urgent and Confidential.*

"Wow," Phoebe said. "How did this get here?"

"Beats me," I said. "Let's see what's in there." I reached for the envelope, but Phoebe hugged it to her chest and twisted away from me.

"Can't you *read*?" she scolded me. "It says it's confidential."

"Fine," I told her. "Keep it to yourself. See if I care."

Phoebe looked flustered and excited. "What should we do?" she asked.

"Just throw it back on the ground," I told her. "It probably isn't important."

"It's *urgent*, you big dummy," Phoebe said, looking at the front of the envelope again. "We've got to get this to her. I know where she lives—it's not far from here."

"No way," I said. "I've got to get to school. I don't have time to run around all over town."

"*Fine*," Phoebe sniffed. "I'll go by myself. Someone around here has to be responsible."

"Suit yourself," I told her.

Phoebe glared at me a few seconds and then took off running. I watched her head down the block and turn down the street where Dr. Griffith lives.

I stood there a while, enjoying the moment. I pictured Phoebe knocking on the door and giving Dr. Griffith the letter. I could imagine her standing there, grinning like an idiot, while Dr. Griffith read the letter inside and then looked her over. It was rich.

I look a deep breath and smiled up at the beautiful billowing clouds. "Life is good," I said aloud and then headed up the street toward school.

The rest of the day was just as good. My column came out in the newspaper without a word being changed, and we only had to do sit-ups in school for the Physical Fitness Exam. I'm good at sit-ups. I was well on the way to joining the governor's elite ranks.

I headed home that day with a song in my heart and my backpack slung over one shoulder. Fridays always felt good. I had a whole weekend ahead of me with no homework. I carried my gym clothes rolled up like a football. Every few steps I'd toss them in the air and catch them.

When I got to my house, I noticed that Phoebe's garage door was open.

"Hey, Willie," Phoebe said. "Come on over here. I need some help with this."

I grinned. "So how was Dr. Griffith?" I asked. I stepped into the dark garage.

"Very funny," Phoebe said. "It took me so long to convince her I wasn't crazy, I was late for school." It took a few seconds for my eyes to adjust to the dim light, but when they did, I saw Phoebe bent over a large cardboard box.

"It's too heavy for me," she said. "I need to put it up there." She pointed to a shelf over her father's workbench.

I grinned. This was obviously some kind of set-up. "Yeah, right," I said. "There's a hole in the bottom of the box and it'll spill glue all over my shoes when I pick it up, right?"

"There's nothing wrong with the box," Phoebe said. "It's just too heavy for me."

I smiled at her. "You think I'm an idiot, don't you?"

"True," Phoebe said. "But not because of this. Now stop being so silly and help me out."

I gingerly stepped up to the box and tapped it with my toe. Phoebe put her hands on her hips. "It's just art supplies, you big dope," she told me. "Look inside if you don't believe me."

I bent down and slowly pulled back the flaps of the box, making sure my face was clear in case something flew out. But Phoebe was telling the truth. The box was full of pencil sets, brushes, and paints.

Phoebe rolled her eyes. "Look, will you put it up there already?"

I looked up at the shelf. "Oh, I get it," I said. "The shelf will fall, and all that stuff will land on me."

"It's *just* a *shelf*," Phoebe said, her voice brimming with exasperation. "I just need you to put the box on the shelf. Got it? That's *all*."

"So you expect me to believe there's nothing wrong with the box or the shelf?"

"Of *course* there isn't."

"Promise?"

"*Yes*, I promise," Phoebe said completely aggravated. "Will you get *on* with it?"

I still only half believed her. I handed her my gym clothes and carefully picked the box up. It *was* pretty heavy, and the fact that I hadn't taken off my backpack made it worse. I hefted it over to the workbench and struggled to lift it up to the shelf. With a groan, I managed to push it into place.

"*There*," Phoebe said. "Was that so hard?" She tossed me my gym clothes. "You're getting totally paranoid, Willie."

Sunday night after church, I threw my gym clothes in the washer and set it to the regular cycle. I didn't have any homework due, and my *Ask Amy* column was done for the week. I didn't have a worry in the world.

I went in the living room to watch television. About an hour later Amanda called me from the dining room doorway.

"Hey, Willie," she said. "I need to wash some stuff. Okay if I move your load to the dryer?"

I'd completely forgotten about the wash. "Sure," I said. "Help yourself." *Cool*, I thought. *I don't even have to get off the sofa to put my gym clothes in the dryer.* I put my hands behind my head and my heels on the coffee table. This had been a great weekend.

"Uh, Willie?" Amanda called from the dining room again. "You might want to come look at this."

"Can it wait?"

"Not really," she said. "And I just want you to know I had nothing to do with it."

I got up from the sofa and followed Amanda through the dining room and kitchen to the laundry room. The washer's lid was open. Amanda reached into the washer and pulled out a dripping pink T-shirt. She held it up by the shoulders.

"How did your T-shirt get in with my gym clothes?" I asked.

"It's not *my* shirt," she said. She turned the shirt around. On the front it read GLENFIELD MIDDLE SCHOOL. It took me a few seconds to realize what the shirt was.

"Oh no!" I gasped. I reached into the washer and pulled out my pink gym shorts and two pink socks. "What happened?"

"You must have washed them with something red," Amanda told me.

I held my soggy, pink gym clothes over the open washer and peered inside. "There's nothing else in there," I told her. "How did this happen?"

"Don't look at me," Amanda said. "*I* didn't do anything. You must have put *something* red in there."

"No," I said. "Imposs—"

Just then it hit me. Standing there holding my dripping pink gym clothes, I knew the whole story: Phoebe had asked me to move that box for her on Friday afternoon. I'd been so paranoid about the box, I didn't keep an eye on *her*! She must have slipped a cake of red paint into my rolled up gym clothes. My mind reeled. I put my free hand on the cool metal of the washing machine to steady myself.

I didn't know what to feel. I was furious, but on another level I was oddly impressed. Phoebe knew I brought my gym clothes home on Friday and washed them myself. She'd thought of the perfect way to get me to hand them over to her without giving it a second thought. She'd even gotten *me* to put back the box where she'd gotten the red paint. *That girl was good!*

I stayed up until after midnight washing and rewashing my gym clothes, but they were still bright pink when I gave up and put them in the dryer.

On Monday afternoon, when I was in the locker room suiting up for gym, Felix couldn't stop laughing at my pink gym suit. I'd stalled until everyone else was gone before I'd changed clothes. It was just too embarrassing.

"Phoebe did that?" Felix said, once he'd managed to stop laughing long enough to get the words out.

"Yep," I said. "She got me bad." I tucked my pink shirt into my pink shorts. "Well, look on the bright side," I said. "At least Big Ernie is safe today. With *me* dressed like this, Leonard Grubb isn't going to pay much attention to *him*."

Felix started laughing again. I closed my street clothes in the locker and clicked the lock shut. This was going to be a long gym class.

"So are you going to get Phoebe back?" Felix wanted to know. "Are you hatching some kind of prank to pull on her? I'd be happy to assist." He seemed to be enjoying this practical joke war between me and Phoebe—especially since he was never the victim.

"I've already thought of one," I told him. "But it's a one man job."

I tied my last shoelace and straightened up. Outside, 29 fellow students and one coach were waiting to make fun of me. I puffed up my cheeks and blew out the air. "Well, here goes," I said. I headed for the door. Felix fell in beside me.

"I don't know about the Governor's Physical Fitness Team," Felix said, putting one arm around my shoulder, "but if he has a ballet troupe, you're a shoo-in."

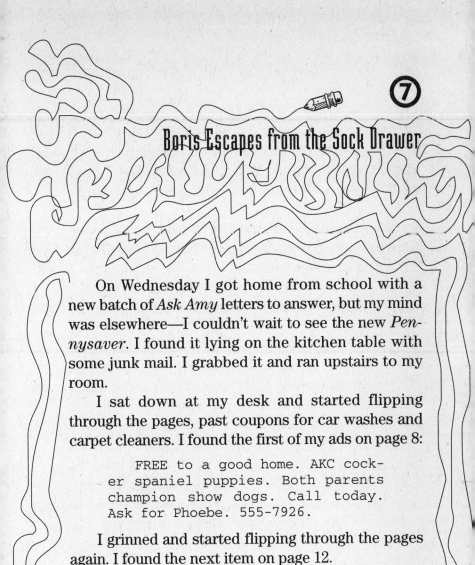

Boris Escapes from the Sock Drawer

On Wednesday I got home from school with a new batch of *Ask Amy* letters to answer, but my mind was elsewhere—I couldn't wait to see the new *Pennysaver*. I found it lying on the kitchen table with some junk mail. I grabbed it and ran upstairs to my room.

I sat down at my desk and started flipping through the pages, past coupons for car washes and carpet cleaners. I found the first of my ads on page 8:

```
FREE to a good home. AKC cock-
er spaniel puppies. Both parents
champion show dogs. Call today.
Ask for Phoebe. 555-7926.
```

I grinned and started flipping through the pages again. I found the next item on page 12.

```
As a public service I am offer-
ing FREE baby-sitting to all Glen-
```

```
field   residents.   Limited   slots
still   available.   Call 555-7926.
Ask for Phoebe.
```

Five minutes later I'd found nine of the 10 ads. I was looking for the last one when I heard the phone ring next door. I started laughing. I got up, went to my window, and slid it open. I forced myself to stop laughing so I could listen. It wasn't easy.

Someone in Phoebe's house picked up the phone midway through the third ring. "*Phoebe*," I heard Mrs. Snyder call. "It's for you."

I staggered over to my bed and collapsed laughing.

The phone at Phoebe's house didn't stop ringing all afternoon. That night, while I was trying to work on my *Ask Amy* column, it rang about every 10 minutes. I tried to think of a reply to the first letter, but each time Phoebe's phone rang, I held my breath and waited. Then, when someone finally called out "*Phoebe*, it's for you again," I about fell off my chair laughing.

All I could picture was Phoebe on the phone saying "No, I *don't* want to trade a 1932 Mercedes Benz for your Toyota pick-up," or "No, I'm *not* selling a complete Beanie Babies collection; I don't even *have* a collection." In fact, I laughed so much, it took me nearly an hour to answer the first letter.

Dear Amy,

There's this guy I really like. I see him every day at school. He's really popular, and he doesn't even know I'm alive. He's in two of my classes, but we've never even talked. I guess I'm kind of shy. I don't think he even knows my name. How can I get him to notice me?

Kajyo Yamamoto

I knew Kajyo; we both had Mr. Keefer first period. She was pretty but very quiet and shy. She sat in a corner seat and hardly ever talked. It was easy to forget she was there. I pictured her sitting there in class bent over the notes she was taking. I wished there was something I could tell her that would help her come out of her shell.

Dear Bashful,

If a person doesn't hear you whisper, it's time to shout.

I know it's hard to get people's attention when you're shy. If the guy you like doesn't notice you, you need to think of some dramatic way to get his attention. The more dramatic it is, the more likely you are to get (and keep) his attention.

Amy

Okay, it wasn't perfect. Maybe if I wasn't drooling on myself with laughter half the time, I could have done a better job. But when I read it over, it looked pretty good to me. And what harm could it do?

I turned over the second letter.

Dear Amy,

I'm tired of being pushed around. A certain bully at this school has it in for me. He teases me and picks on me. I spend my whole day running away from him and hiding. I can't go on living this way, but I don't have the guts to stand up to him. What should I do?

Ernie Pignatello

My mouth dropped open. Big Ernie wanted my advice on how to handle Crusher Grubb—and I knew just what to tell him. This was the perfect opportunity! I thought of Ernie—big *muscular* Ernie. I thought of all the cruel things Leonard had done to him in the last few weeks. I thought of what *I'd* do to Leonard if I had muscles like Ernie's!

I know the Bible says we should turn the other cheek, but right then there was nothing I wanted more than to have Big Ernie pound Crusher Grubb. I wanted revenge. When I first started writing the *Ask Amy* column, I tried to give advice from the Bible when I could. But now I was hot stuff. I was advisor to the stars. Now I just thought about what *I'd* like to see happen. I was relying on my *own* wisdom.

I got a clean sheet of paper and sharpened my pencil. I looked up at the ceiling, trying to formulate a good first line. The phone next door rang. I burst out laughing so hard I dropped my pencil and it rolled under my desk.

It must have taken me another hour to finish. Every time I got on a roll, Phoebe's phone would ring and I'd be seized by a fit of laughing. By the time I got done with my answer, there were tears in my eyes.

Dear Hounded,

It sounds like you are living in a difficult situation, and it sounds like you think you have no power to change it. But few of us know what we can do until we're tested. We hear every day about average people who did something remarkable when the situation demanded it. They didn't know they had it in them—but they did all along.

You have no idea what you can do till you try. I challenge you to stand up to this bully. I suspect that you have all kinds of untapped potential. Have courage! Your situation isn't as hopeless as you think. The next time that bully comes up to you, get up in his face and tell him that if he doesn't leave you alone, you're going to squash him like a bug.

Amy

I read my answer over. I hoped it was persuasive enough. If I wasn't big enough to beat up Crusher myself, I hoped this letter would give me that satisfaction indirectly. I turned to the fourth and final letter.

Dear Amy,

   I have an incredible fear of hieghts. It's
really driving me crazy. I can't even look out
a second story window without feeling faint. A
few weeks ago I had to fly in a plain, and I
was so scared I nearly fainted. In a couple of
months I will have to fly in a plain again, and
I can't stop worrying about it. How can I get
over my acrophobia?

                          Boris Dragas

Boris? I thought. The little man who lived in
Phoebe's sock drawer? Phoebe *had* to be behind this.
Even as the phone next door was ringing off the hook,
Phoebe was already at work on her next prank!

   I read the letter again. It was clearly from Phoebe.
Why would Boris Dragas misspell the word *heights*
and use the wrong word for *plane*—yet get the word
acrophobia right? Obviously Phoebe—who took six-
teenth place in the state spelling bee championship—
was trying to convince me it wasn't her. It was pretty
transparent. And who ever heard of a kid named
Boris anyway?

   I sat there a moment, trying to think of what I
should do. I knew Phoebe was up to something, but I
couldn't figure out what. Phoebe was a much better
prankster than I'd given her credit for. It seemed
safest to play along and see where this thing went.

   I got out a sheet of paper and began my response.

As I folded the paper back up, I glanced down the hall to see if Felix or Sam were coming. It was then I saw him. Vincent Espinoza, fallen star athlete, was heading down the hall in my direction. I backed up against the wall and held the paper up in front of my face like a detective in an old movie. Vincent made a bee-line for the newspaper table and grabbed a copy.

As I peeked over my paper, Vincent ripped open his and found my column. He folded it back and began to read. I was so close I could see his eyes move back and forth across the column. He started nodding his head a little. A faint smile spread across his face. He turned and entered the cafeteria with the paper tucked under his arm. My heart was pounding.

When I went in the cafeteria, Sam was already eating. I got my tray and joined her at the table. In a few minutes Felix sat down as well.

"Did you see my ketchup story?" Felix asked. He didn't sound pleased.

Once again, I'd been so concerned about my own column, I'd forgotten to look for Felix's article. "No," I told him. "I didn't get a chance." I got my copy of the paper and flipped through it. I scanned the back page.

"They cut my story completely," Felix said.

I thought how disappointed he must be. His first story got cut down to a paragraph, and his second didn't make it in the paper at all.

"Gee, Felix," I said. "That's too bad. Maybe there just wasn't enough room. Remember, they had to make room for the big story on …" I glanced over the first page for a big, important story. "… the seventh-grade car wash."

"They're trying to silence me," Felix said.

"Sure," I said. "That's it. They couldn't handle that kind of controversy."

"Oh, *please*," Sam burst in. "Don't encourage him." Felix turned to look at her.

"Felix," Sam said. "Your stories are boring."

Felix's mouth dropped open. He just sat there blinking. I felt bad for him.

"*Ketchup*?" Sam said. "*Parking lots*? I can see your next headline: Grass Keeps Growing Despite Expensive Weekly Mowing: Who Is To Blame?"

It caught me off guard; I laughed. Felix shot me an angry look.

"The Ketchup Scandal was a good story," Felix sulked. "They shouldn't have cut it."

"Look," Sam said. "If you want to end up on the front page, you've got to find a scoop. You've got to find a story people care about—something important to *them*." She gestured around at all the kids in the cafeteria. "You've got to write something these guys want to read."

"Like what?"

"Oh, I don't know," Sam said. She tucked her blonde hair behind her ears. "Remember that article Kelly Pham wrote about how much money boys' ath-

Dear Fearful,

The only way to truly conquer a fear is to face it head-on. When you fall off a horse the thing to do is climb right back in the saddle.

Here's what you need to do: Buy a good rope and go climb a cliff. Get a tough nylon rope, at least 100 feet long. Any good hardware store will have what you need. For a good cliff, I recommend the old quarry out on the interstate.

Once you've gone up and down the cliff a few times, I'm sure the airplane ride won't seem nearly so scary.

Amy

I was writing the *m* in Amy when the phone next door rang again. It took me four minutes to write the *y*.

When I dropped this batch of letters off in Miss Pell's room, I thought I'd better give her an explanation.

"You might find my advice a little odd this week," I told her. "You see, a friend of mine wrote this letter pretending to be someone else. It's all part of a series of practical jokes."

Miss Pell didn't say a word. She just looked at me over her glasses for a few seconds and then opened the envelope and pulled out the letters. She read Phoebe's fake letter first. I saw her eyebrow twitch four times—once for each of Phoebe's intentional spelling errors. Then she turned to my answer. As she read, I watched her eyebrow. It didn't move—I must have done okay, despite last night's frequent attacks of convulsive laughter.

When she finished reading, she looked at me over her glasses again. "I'm not sure I like the idea of our school newspaper becoming a forum for practical jokes," she told me. "Were there any other letters this week?"

"No," I told her. "Just these three."

Miss Pell looked at both letters again. She sighed. "You're *certain* this is a joke?" she asked.

"Positive," I said.

"We'll run the letters this week because we have space to fill," she announced. "But I don't want you to make a habit of this, Wilbur Plummet."

I shook my head. "No way," I said—just to see her eyebrow jump.

On Friday I picked up a copy of the *Gopher Gazette* outside the cafeteria. This was the issue that would carry my advice to Vincent Espinoza, so I was pretty excited. I didn't even wait to go inside to look at my column; I opened the paper right there, with all the students passing around me into the cafeteria. My letter to Vincent was exactly the way I wrote it.

As I folded the paper back up, I glanced down the hall to see if Felix or Sam were coming. It was then I saw him. Vincent Espinoza, fallen star athlete, was heading down the hall in my direction. I backed up against the wall and held the paper up in front of my face like a detective in an old movie. Vincent made a bee-line for the newspaper table and grabbed a copy.

As I peeked over my paper, Vincent ripped open his and found my column. He folded it back and began to read. I was so close I could see his eyes move back and forth across the column. He started nodding his head a little. A faint smile spread across his face. He turned and entered the cafeteria with the paper tucked under his arm. My heart was pounding.

When I went in the cafeteria, Sam was already eating. I got my tray and joined her at the table. In a few minutes Felix sat down as well.

"Did you see my ketchup story?" Felix asked. He didn't sound pleased.

Once again, I'd been so concerned about my own column, I'd forgotten to look for Felix's article. "No," I told him. "I didn't get a chance." I got my copy of the paper and flipped through it. I scanned the back page.

"They cut my story completely," Felix said.

I thought how disappointed he must be. His first story got cut down to a paragraph, and his second didn't make it in the paper at all.

"Gee, Felix," I said. "That's too bad. Maybe there just wasn't enough room. Remember, they had to make room for the big story on …" I glanced over the first page for a big, important story. "… the seventh-grade car wash."

"They're trying to silence me," Felix said.

"Sure," I said. "That's it. They couldn't handle that kind of controversy."

"Oh, *please*," Sam burst in. "Don't encourage him." Felix turned to look at her.

"Felix," Sam said. "Your stories are boring."

Felix's mouth dropped open. He just sat there blinking. I felt bad for him.

"*Ketchup*?" Sam said. "*Parking lots*? I can see your next headline: Grass Keeps Growing Despite Expensive Weekly Mowing: Who Is To Blame?"

It caught me off guard; I laughed. Felix shot me an angry look.

"The Ketchup Scandal was a good story," Felix sulked. "They shouldn't have cut it."

"Look," Sam said. "If you want to end up on the front page, you've got to find a scoop. You've got to find a story people care about—something important to *them*." She gestured around at all the kids in the cafeteria. "You've got to write something these guys want to read."

"Like what?"

"Oh, I don't know," Sam said. She tucked her blonde hair behind her ears. "Remember that article Kelly Pham wrote about how much money boys' ath-

She twisted around to look at me. "I *love* baseball," she said. "You think I know nothing about sports, but you're wrong."

Who was she trying to impress? "Oh yeah?" I said. "What's your all-time favorite baseball team?"

"The Houston Colts."

I snorted. She was pathetic. "The Colts are a *football* team," I snipped. "And they're *not* from Houston. Houston's team is the Astros."

"Houston's team was the Colt 45s until 1965," Phoebe told me. "Everyone just called them the Colts for short."

I glanced over at Sam. Baseball is her sport. "She's right," Sam said. "That was before they built the Astrodome."

I felt pretty stupid. I guess I should have known better than to assume there was anything Phoebe didn't know.

I looked out at the field. The Gophers were warming up. Vincent stood near home plate, holding a bat across his shoulders. He was looking out at the fence in center field.

You can do it, Vincent, I thought. *Just relax and visualize that ball sailing over that fence.* My stomach felt knotted. I think I was more nervous about the game than Vincent was—which I guess was a good thing.

"Earth to Willie," Phoebe said. I looked down at her. She was twisted around looking up at me again.

letics got compared to the girls? That was a real scoop. Kids were talking about that for weeks."

"Yeah," Felix protested. "But that was big news."

"It wasn't news at all until Kelly wrote the story," Sam pointed out.

While Sam and Felix bickered, I looked around the cafeteria for Vincent. He was sitting at a table against the back wall. He had the paper spread out in front of him on the table. His chin was in his hands and he was staring into middle distance like he was thinking.

Felix and Sam were still arguing, but I interrupted them. "Is there a baseball game today?" I asked.

"You mean a Gophers' game?" Sam asked.

"Yeah."

"I think so," Felix said. "No one goes to the games anymore. It's too depressing. We'd have to win every game for the rest of the season just to make it to the playoffs."

"I'd like to go today," I said. "I gave Vincent some advice in today's paper. I want to see if it makes any difference."

Sam looked at Felix and then back at me. "I'm in," she said.

Felix shrugged. "Okay," he said. "Me too. I'd like to see Vincent play. It always cheers me up to see someone worse off than me."

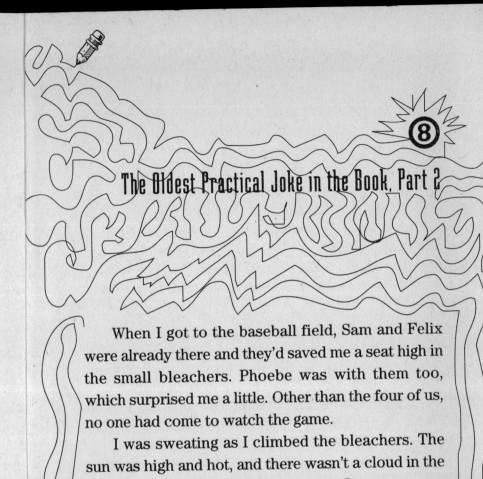

When I got to the baseball field, Sam and Felix were already there and they'd saved me a seat high in the small bleachers. Phoebe was with them too, which surprised me a little. Other than the four of us, no one had come to watch the game.

I was sweating as I climbed the bleachers. The sun was high and hot, and there wasn't a cloud in the sky. But I was also sweating because I was nervous. Vincent had asked me for advice, and I'd given him some. What if he followed it and had as bad a game as ever? I felt responsible.

I took a seat next to Felix and behind Sam and Phoebe. I leaned back on the bench behind me. "What are you doing here, Phoeb?" I asked her. "You don't like baseball. Trying to get away from all those phone calls?"

"With your red hair and fair skin you should limit your exposure to sunlight," she told me. "Why don't you put on some of my sunscreen?" She had this weird look on her face, like she was smiling but trying her hardest not to.

Suddenly everything became clear. *That's* why she was here. She wasn't here to watch the game. She was here to get even with me for all the ads I'd put in the *Pennysaver*. She held out the plastic bottle of sunscreen.

Was it possible she didn't know this was the oldest practical joke in the book? Did she *really* think I was going to fall for mayonnaise in the sunscreen bottle? She might know baseball, but *I* knew pranks.

To tell you the truth, after the pink gym clothes trick, I was a little disappointed to see her try so lame a prank—but after all she *was* only 9. It wasn't like I was engaged in a battle of wits with Stephen Hawking.

I looked at Sam and Felix. They had a glint in their eyes, as if Phoebe had told them what she was up to and made them promise not to tell.

I squinted up at the glaring sun. "You know, you're right," I said, straight-faced. "Let me have some of that stuff."

I took the bottle and flipped up the cap. Phoebe looked like she was about to burst out laughing. The poor girl actually thought I was going to rub that stuff all over me!

I decided I'd make a big show of it. I'd turn the trick around on her. I'd *pretend* I was falling for it, and then I'd pull the rug out. And I'd do it with flair!

I pulled up the sleeves on my T-shirt. I rubbed my palm on my shorts and then held it under plastic bottle, like I was about to give it a squeeze. Phoebe's eyes got wide.

I grinned at her. "You're not going to get me that easy," I told her. "Mayonnaise in the sunscreen bottle. The oldest trick in the book." I stuck out my tongue and squeezed the bottle so hard most of the mayonnaise squirted in my mouth. I started laughing.

Phoebe, Sam, and Felix burst out laughing too. For a second I didn't know *what* they were laughing at—and then the horrible taste hit me. It wasn't mayonnaise. My mouth was full of 40 SPF sunscreen. I started gagging. It was the worst taste imaginable—a hundred times worse than my father's chili.

"Sunscreen in the sunscreen bottle," I heard Felix say. "The second oldest trick in the book."

I scrambled to the top of the bleachers and bent over the back. I spat out all the sunscreen I could. It was all I could do to keep my lunch down. I stuck my tongue out and wiped it with the sleeve of my T-shirt. The taste was so bad my ears ached and my eyes watered. I could hear Phoebe, Sam, and Felix laughing behind me. I'd have told them all to shut up, but I had completely lost the power of speech.

I climbed down from the bleachers and jogged to the drinking fountain behind the backstop. My eyes were watering so bad, it was hard to see where I was going. I rinsed my mouth out and gargled about a dozen times, but the taste lingered.

When I got back to my seat I was exhausted, like I'd just finished the mile run in the Governor's Physical Fitness Test. Phoebe, Sam, and Felix weren't in much better shape than I was. They were laughing so hard, they were having trouble breathing. It took a few minutes, but we all eventually regained our composure.

"You should have seen your face," Sam told me. "I wish I'd brought a camera."

"You've got to admit she got you good," Felix said.

Phoebe twisted around to look at me again. "All kidding aside," Phoebe said. "You *should* put on some sunscreen."

She held out the bottle to me again. I must have looked like she was holding out a cobra, because Sam and Felix started laughing again.

"It's okay," Phoebe said. "Just read the warning label: 'For external use only.' "

Sam and Felix laughed even harder. I took the bottle and looked at it suspiciously. Maybe I was paranoid, but what if this time it was *really* full of mayonnaise? She could easily have switched bottles while I was at the drinking fountain. I felt weary and beaten. I was no match for Phoebe.

I stared at the bottle in my hand. I twisted off the cap and sniffed it. Sam and Felix started laughing again—so hard they looked in danger of falling through the bleachers. It *was* sunscreen.

In a way it was too late: My face was redder than any sunburn, but I squirted some sunscreen on my palm and rubbed it into my arms until it disappeared.

In the bottom of the first inning, the Gophers came up to bat. Neither team had scored. The Gophers' lead off hitter got to first base on a walk, and the next two got out with pop flies, but I wasn't really watching the game. The whole time I kept my eye on Vincent—in the dugout, on deck while he loosened up.

When Vincent came up to the plate, his teammates didn't call out any encouragement—it was clear the losing streak had taken a toll on them. They all sat sullenly on the bench with their heads down. All the hopes and dreams of the early season had vanished. Coach Askew paced sullenly in front of the dugout. It was like he didn't even want to *look* at Vincent.

Vincent tapped the side of his cleats with the bat. The outfielders on the other team moved in, but Vincent didn't seem to notice. When he took his position at the plate he gazed out at the center field fence—just like I'd told him to.

letics got compared to the girls? That was a real scoop. Kids were talking about that for weeks."

"Yeah," Felix protested. "But that was big news."

"It wasn't news at all until Kelly wrote the story," Sam pointed out.

While Sam and Felix bickered, I looked around the cafeteria for Vincent. He was sitting at a table against the back wall. He had the paper spread out in front of him on the table. His chin was in his hands and he was staring into middle distance like he was thinking.

Felix and Sam were still arguing, but I interrupted them. "Is there a baseball game today?" I asked.

"You mean a Gophers' game?" Sam asked.

"Yeah."

"I think so," Felix said. "No one goes to the games anymore. It's too depressing. We'd have to win every game for the rest of the season just to make it to the playoffs."

"I'd like to go today," I said. "I gave Vincent some advice in today's paper. I want to see if it makes any difference."

Sam looked at Felix and then back at me. "I'm in," she said.

Felix shrugged. "Okay," he said. "Me too. I'd like to see Vincent play. It always cheers me up to see someone worse off than me."

When I got to the baseball field, Sam and Felix were already there and they'd saved me a seat high in the small bleachers. Phoebe was with them too, which surprised me a little. Other than the four of us, no one had come to watch the game.

I was sweating as I climbed the bleachers. The sun was high and hot, and there wasn't a cloud in the sky. But I was also sweating because I was nervous. Vincent had asked me for advice, and I'd given him some. What if he followed it and had as bad a game as ever? I felt responsible.

I took a seat next to Felix and behind Sam and Phoebe. I leaned back on the bench behind me. "What are you doing here, Phoeb?" I asked her. "You don't like baseball. Trying to get away from all those phone calls?"

She twisted around to look at me. "I *love* baseball," she said. "You think I know nothing about sports, but you're wrong."

Who was she trying to impress? "Oh yeah?" I said. "What's your all-time favorite baseball team?"

"The Houston Colts."

I snorted. She was pathetic. "The Colts are a *football* team," I snipped. "And they're *not* from Houston. Houston's team is the Astros."

"Houston's team was the Colt 45s until 1965," Phoebe told me. "Everyone just called them the Colts for short."

I glanced over at Sam. Baseball is her sport. "She's right," Sam said. "That was before they built the Astrodome."

I felt pretty stupid. I guess I should have known better than to assume there was anything Phoebe didn't know.

I looked out at the field. The Gophers were warming up. Vincent stood near home plate, holding a bat across his shoulders. He was looking out at the fence in center field.

You can do it, Vincent, I thought. *Just relax and visualize that ball sailing over that fence.* My stomach felt knotted. I think I was more nervous about the game than Vincent was—which I guess was a good thing.

"Earth to Willie," Phoebe said. I looked down at her. She was twisted around looking up at me again.

"With your red hair and fair skin you should limit your exposure to sunlight," she told me. "Why don't you put on some of my sunscreen?" She had this weird look on her face, like she was smiling but trying her hardest not to.

Suddenly everything became clear. *That's* why she was here. She wasn't here to watch the game. She was here to get even with me for all the ads I'd put in the *Pennysaver.* She held out the plastic bottle of sunscreen.

Was it possible she didn't know this was the oldest practical joke in the book? Did she *really* think I was going to fall for mayonnaise in the sunscreen bottle? She might know baseball, but *I* knew pranks.

To tell you the truth, after the pink gym clothes trick, I was a little disappointed to see her try so lame a prank—but after all she *was* only 9. It wasn't like I was engaged in a battle of wits with Stephen Hawking.

I looked at Sam and Felix. They had a glint in their eyes, as if Phoebe had told them what she was up to and made them promise not to tell.

I squinted up at the glaring sun. "You know, you're right," I said, straight-faced. "Let me have some of that stuff."

I took the bottle and flipped up the cap. Phoebe looked like she was about to burst out laughing. The poor girl actually thought I was going to rub that stuff all over me!

I decided I'd make a big show of it. I'd turn the trick around on her. I'd *pretend* I was falling for it, and then I'd pull the rug out. And I'd do it with flair!

I pulled up the sleeves on my T-shirt. I rubbed my palm on my shorts and then held it under plastic bottle, like I was about to give it a squeeze. Phoebe's eyes got wide.

I grinned at her. "You're not going to get me that easy," I told her. "Mayonnaise in the sunscreen bottle. The oldest trick in the book." I stuck out my tongue and squeezed the bottle so hard most of the mayonnaise squirted in my mouth. I started laughing.

Phoebe, Sam, and Felix burst out laughing too. For a second I didn't know *what* they were laughing at—and then the horrible taste hit me. It wasn't mayonnaise. My mouth was full of 40 SPF sunscreen. I started gagging. It was the worst taste imaginable—a hundred times worse than my father's chili.

"Sunscreen in the sunscreen bottle," I heard Felix say. "The second oldest trick in the book."

I scrambled to the top of the bleachers and bent over the back. I spat out all the sunscreen I could. It was all I could do to keep my lunch down. I stuck my tongue out and wiped it with the sleeve of my T-shirt. The taste was so bad my ears ached and my eyes watered. I could hear Phoebe, Sam, and Felix laughing behind me. I'd have told them all to shut up, but I had completely lost the power of speech.

I climbed down from the bleachers and jogged to the drinking fountain behind the backstop. My eyes were watering so bad, it was hard to see where I was going. I rinsed my mouth out and gargled about a dozen times, but the taste lingered.

When I got back to my seat I was exhausted, like I'd just finished the mile run in the Governor's Physical Fitness Test. Phoebe, Sam, and Felix weren't in much better shape than I was. They were laughing so hard, they were having trouble breathing. It took a few minutes, but we all eventually regained our composure.

"You should have seen your face," Sam told me. "I wish I'd brought a camera."

"You've got to admit she got you good," Felix said.

Phoebe twisted around to look at me again. "All kidding aside," Phoebe said. "You *should* put on some sunscreen."

She held out the bottle to me again. I must have looked like she was holding out a cobra, because Sam and Felix started laughing again.

"It's okay," Phoebe said. "Just read the warning label: 'For external use only.' "

Sam and Felix laughed even harder. I took the bottle and looked at it suspiciously. Maybe I was paranoid, but what if this time it was *really* full of mayonnaise? She could easily have switched bottles while I was at the drinking fountain. I felt weary and beaten. I was no match for Phoebe.

I stared at the bottle in my hand. I twisted off the cap and sniffed it. Sam and Felix started laughing again—so hard they looked in danger of falling through the bleachers. It *was* sunscreen.

In a way it was too late: My face was redder than any sunburn, but I squirted some sunscreen on my palm and rubbed it into my arms until it disappeared.

In the bottom of the first inning, the Gophers came up to bat. Neither team had scored. The Gophers' lead off hitter got to first base on a walk, and the next two got out with pop flies, but I wasn't really watching the game. The whole time I kept my eye on Vincent—in the dugout, on deck while he loosened up.

When Vincent came up to the plate, his teammates didn't call out any encouragement—it was clear the losing streak had taken a toll on them. They all sat sullenly on the bench with their heads down. All the hopes and dreams of the early season had vanished. Coach Askew paced sullenly in front of the dugout. It was like he didn't even want to *look* at Vincent.

Vincent tapped the side of his cleats with the bat. The outfielders on the other team moved in, but Vincent didn't seem to notice. When he took his position at the plate he gazed out at the center field fence—just like I'd told him to.

Remember, I thought. *You love this game. You've hit that ball thousands of times. There's no pressure.*

Vincent let the first two pitches go—a strike and a ball. The smile never left his face. When the next pitch came, it seemed like the world suddenly went in slow motion. The pitch was a fast ball right over the middle of the plate. Vincent's shoulder dropped into the swing, and the bat came around in a sweeping circle. There was the delicious *ping* of the ball hitting the aluminum bat. The ball rocketed high into center field.

The other team's center fielder sprinted toward the fence, but jogged to a stop when he saw that the ball would easily clear it. I saw the white ball bounce twice on the hill behind center field and disappear on the other side.

Vincent Espinoza was back!

When the game ended, with the Gophers winning seven to three, the team hooted and hollered and dog-piled on Vincent. I sat up there in the bleachers with goose bumps on my arms while Felix, Sam, and Phoebe cheered—it felt, in a way, like all this applause was for me.

The next Wednesday afternoon, Felix called me up and asked me if he could come over. He said he'd been working for a few days on a new feature story and he wanted me to look at it.

I rolled my eyes. I could just imagine the headline: Boys' Gym Showers Not Hot Enough: Students Risk Colds, Flu.

"I've got to write my *own* column tonight," I told him. "I don't think I could give your article the kind of attention it needs. Maybe you could call Sam."

"Oh, yes," Felix said, his voice full of sarcasm. "And you've also got *gymnastics* to worry about. I know a lame excuse when I hear one. I'm coming over." He hung up the phone.

There was nothing I could do now. I'd have to read whatever dumb story Felix came up with this time, and then I'd have to think of polite things to say about it. I went into the living room and switched on the TV. Five minutes later the doorbell rang.

"I think this is it," he told me standing in the doorway. "I think this is the one that will actually end up on the front page." He handed me a couple of computer-printed pages.

"Well, the important thing is that you do your best," I said. It's what Dad sometimes tells me when my report card isn't so hot. By the look on Felix's face, I could tell he didn't find the expression any more encouraging than I usually do.

"I'm serious," he said. "I've been thinking about what Sam said. About how I should find something the kids at school care about. Call me and tell me what you think."

"Sure," I told him, trying my best to sound excited. "I'd be happy to."

Felix turned and jogged down the porch steps to where his bike lay on my front lawn. As he picked it up he smiled at me. "I know you think this story will stink," he said. "But it's going to surprise you."

When Felix pedaled away, I pushed the door shut and looked at his headline: Star Athlete Credits Mysterious Writer. I switched off the television and sat down on the sofa.

Star Athlete Credits Mysterious Writer

There is no sports story more interesting than a comeback. There's nothing that stirs the imagination like someone who gets knocked down, but who rises to his feet—just before the final count—and comes back to win the fight.

One such fighter is Vincent Espinoza, cleanup hitter for the GMS Gophers. During his long batting slump, many of us counted him out. We thought he was through. We thought the Gophers would end their season like they have every year—with a losing record and no invitation to the playoffs. We made fun of Vincent. But no one's laughing now.

During Friday's game, Vincent batted in four runs to beat the Sharks 7 to 3. On Tuesday, against the Highlanders, Vincent hit a home run in the eighth inning that put the Gophers ahead 5 to 4 and won them the game. With four games left in the season, the Gophers have a fighting chance to make it to the playoffs. Now everyone at GMS is once again singing Vincent's praises.

How did this turnaround come about? Vincent credits the mysterious author of the *Ask Amy* column in the *Gopher Gazette.* "I didn't know where to turn," Vincent said. "As a last resort I sent a letter to Amy, and she reminded me why I play baseball in the first place. I owe it all to Amy—I just wish I knew who she was so I could thank her in person."

Will the Gophers make it to the playoffs? Who is the mysterious author who took over the *Ask Amy* column? These are the questions on everyone's lips. We'll soon know the answer to at least one of them.

Maybe it was because the story was partly about me, but it struck me as a pretty good scoop. Maybe this one would get Felix on the front page at last. I felt good for him. After all, like Felix said, we all *do* like a comeback story. And it looked like this might be Felix's comeback story as well.

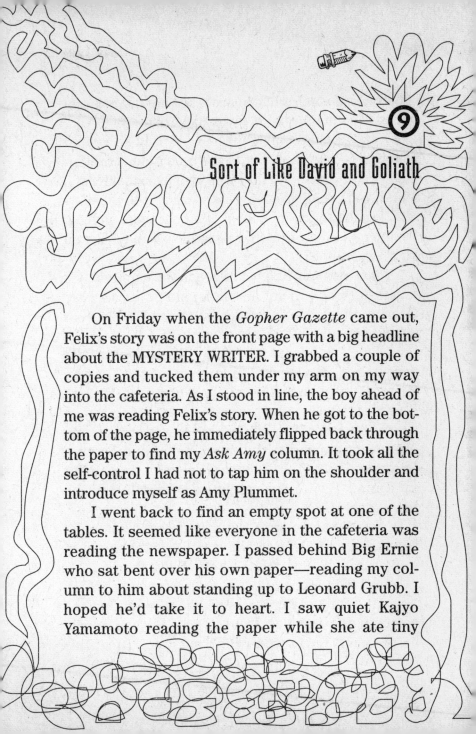

9

Sort of Like David and Goliath

On Friday when the *Gopher Gazette* came out, Felix's story was on the front page with a big headline about the MYSTERY WRITER. I grabbed a couple of copies and tucked them under my arm on my way into the cafeteria. As I stood in line, the boy ahead of me was reading Felix's story. When he got to the bottom of the page, he immediately flipped back through the paper to find my *Ask Amy* column. It took all the self-control I had not to tap him on the shoulder and introduce myself as Amy Plummet.

I went back to find an empty spot at one of the tables. It seemed like everyone in the cafeteria was reading the newspaper. I passed behind Big Ernie who sat bent over his own paper—reading my column to him about standing up to Leonard Grubb. I hoped he'd take it to heart. I saw quiet Kajyo Yamamoto reading the paper while she ate tiny spoonfuls of yogurt. Maybe we'd see her come out of her shell sometime soon. I was on a roll.

I sat down at a table in the very back so I could watch everyone read—all of them no doubt wondering who the Mystery Writer was who had single-handedly saved Glenfield's hopes of making it to the playoffs. I didn't touch my lunch. I just sat there smiling, completely full of myself. I must have looked like an idiot.

I saw Sam and Felix standing in the cafeteria line together. Felix held a whole stack of *Gopher Gazettes*. While they waited in line, a few people went up and congratulated him on his story.

"Wow," Sam said when she finally took a seat next to me. "Everyone's talking about the Mystery Writer. You're almost as big a celebrity as Vincent Espinoza today."

"Did you see it?" Felix asked. He was having trouble setting down his tray because he had about a dozen copies of the *Gopher Gazette* tucked under each arm. "The front page!" he said. "I made it on the front page!"

"You did a good job," Sam admitted. "You found something people care about, and you even put in some suspense with that Mystery Writer thing."

Just then I saw Leonard Grubb walk by with a tray. He was looking for somewhere to sit, but the cafeteria was crowded. Leonard suddenly got a smile and headed over to where Big Ernie was sitting. This was it! First I'd taken care of Vincent, now I was going to take care of a certain school bully!

"You guys, watch this," I told Sam and Felix.

"Watch what?" Sam said.

"Keep an eye on Leonard Grubb," I told her. "You're not going to believe what's going to happen."

Leonard came up behind Big Ernie and grabbed him by the arm. He yanked Ernie out of his seat. Ernie fell backwards into the aisle, and none of us could see him for a few seconds. Leonard sat down in Ernie's place, and the kids on either side of him immediately grabbed their trays and left.

"Come on, Ernie," I said under my breath. "You can do it."

Ernie rose slowly to his feet behind Leonard. He was red-faced and angry. He towered menacingly over Leonard. *Here it comes*! I thought. *This is going to be sweet*!

But suddenly Ernie's posture changed. He stooped. He was suddenly the old Ernie again—Ernie the pushover, Ernie the wimp. Humiliated once again by Leonard Grubb, he turned and shuffled out of the cafeteria.

"That wasn't so hard to believe," Felix said. "I've seen stuff like that before."

"You don't understand," I told him. "He wrote to *Ask Amy*. I told him he should stand up to Crusher." I flipped through the paper to my column and put it down on the table where both Sam and Felix could read it.

I felt kind of mad at Ernie. He hadn't listened to my advice at all. It was exasperating. "I don't understand it," I said. "I thought for *sure* he'd take my advice."

"So Big Ernie wrote this letter?" Felix asked.

"Yes," I said, still in a huff. "*Ernie Pignatello* wrote that letter. Why didn't he take my advice? Wasn't I persuasive enough?"

"I don't think that was the problem," Sam said.

"Well, what *was* the problem, if you're so smart?"

"*That's* not Ernie Pignatello," Sam said.

I felt this sudden falling sensation. "Huh?"

"That's Ernie *Neilson*," she told me. "What is it with you?"

I sat there blinking a few seconds. "He's Ernie *Neilson*?" I managed to say. "Then who's Ernie *Pignatello*?"

"I'll take this one," Felix said to Sam. He turned to me and spoke like he was talking to a 4-year-old. "Ernie Pignatello is that little squirt who keeps borrowing our inferior, off-brand ketchup."

"Wait a minute," I said. I leaned back in my chair trying to piece it all together. "You mean I told that little guy to threaten Leonard Grubb?"

"Take a look," Sam said. She gestured toward the end of the next table.

I hadn't noticed him before because he was so small, but there sat Ernie Pignatello, the school newspaper open on the table in front of him. He was glaring in Leonard Grubb's direction. His lips were moving, though there was no one at the table he seemed to be talking to. He made a fist and pounded it into the palm of his other hand.

"Does that tell you how persuasive you were?" Sam asked me.

"Leonard Grubb will kill him," I said. "I thought I was writing to Big Ernie not *that* little guy."

Ernie Pignatello rose to his feet. His lips were still moving. He started walking slowly in Leonard's direction.

"Maybe he just wants to borrow Leonard's ketchup," Felix said.

Ernie was picking up speed. Both his hands were balled into fists. His jaw was set.

"I've got to *do* something," I said. "I've got to stop him before he gets to Leonard. This is all my fault."

I jumped up and ran. I dashed across the cafeteria and managed to cut Ernie off about 10 feet from where Leonard was sitting. I stood in front of him but he was so intent on Leonard, he didn't seem to notice me.

"Hold on there, Buddy," I told him. I put my hands on his narrow shoulders. "I don't think this is a good idea. Let's talk it over."

Little Ernie never even looked up at me. With my hands on his shoulders I could feel him shaking with rage—with all the anger that had built up over the months of being picked on and bullied by Leonard Grubb.

"This isn't the solution you need," I told him. "Why not just turn the other cheek?" *Now* I was giving good, biblical advice!

Little Ernie's eyes finally rose to mine. It was like he was seeing me for the first time but had no idea who I was.

I smiled.

He didn't.

It was as if all the anger in his eyes was focused on *me* now. It was like *I* was the bully who had pushed him around for so long. I suddenly felt sure he was about to take a swing at *me*.

"Easy there, little guy," I said. I took my hands off his shoulders and stepped back. As near as I can tell, I put my foot down on someone's backpack. At any rate, my ankle twisted under me. I tumbled backwards and slammed into Leonard where he sat at the table. I ended up on my back in the aisle.

I am the only one who knows what happened next—the only one who saw what *really* happened. When I stumbled into Leonard's table, the plastic squeeze bottle of ketchup got knocked over. It fell off the table and rolled into the aisle.

Leonard rose to his feet and stood above me menacingly. "*Get ready for pain, Plummet,*" he snarled. When he stepped into the aisle, he planted his foot square on the ketchup bottle, but he was too furious to notice.

At that same moment, little Ernie Pignatello stepped up behind Leonard and tapped him on the shoulder. Leonard turned to see who was there, and Ernie took a feeble swing at him. From my angle, lying on the floor, it didn't even look like Ernie connected, but Leonard went down like a ton of bricks—he'd slipped on the pool of ketchup underfoot.

Leonard hit the ground face first, and he hit it *hard*. The plastic ketchup bottle skittered under the table and out of sight. Leonard sat up groggily. The wind was knocked out of him. His face was covered with ketchup.

Leonard touched his nose with one hand to see what the wet stuff was, and when his hand came away covered with red, Leonard Grubb fainted right there and then.

I sat up and rubbed my sore ankle. When I looked up at little Ernie Pignatello, he was staring down at his own fist—like he couldn't believe it had actually drawn blood. At that moment, the bell rang.

That afternoon when Felix and I were getting dressed for PE, it was all people could talk about in the locker room: Ernie Pignatello had knocked

Leonard Grubb cold with one bloody punch to the nose. Everyone said Little Ernie had been strutting the halls all afternoon, pushing people around and yelling at them. Instead of ridding the school of its bully, I'd created a new one.

Coach took roll out by the playground fence. We all sat on the grass while he called out the names. I pulled down my sock and rubbed my sore ankle. Since I'd twisted it at lunch, it had turned a pale shade of blue.

"You picked a bad day to sprain your ankle," Felix said. "Today's the final event in the Governor's Physical Fitness Exam—it's the mile run."

"You sure?"

"Yeah," Felix said. "You think you can run on that thing?"

I looked down at my bruised ankle. "I'm about to find out," I told him.

Coach Askew had marked off a mile-long course around the playground. He made us form two lines, and he set us off running in pairs—a new pair every 30 seconds. This way he could time us all in one class period.

Although we weren't really supposed to be racing against each other, that's what it felt like as each pair took off. Felix stood in front of me in line. When he reached the front of the line, he glanced back at me. "Take it easy on that ankle," he told me. Coach gave him the signal, and he took off running along with a kid from the other line.

I put my weight on my sore ankle to test it and winced in pain. I glanced over at the other line to see who I'd be running against. It was Big Ernie.

"Go," Coach barked, looking down at his stop watch. Big Ernie took off in a clumsy gallop, and I fell in limping behind him. As we ran I fell farther behind.

When we got to the corner of the playground fence, Ernie looked back to see where I was. When he saw me running behind him, he looked suddenly astonished. He tripped over his own feet and nearly fell, but then he pushed harder, and the space between us grew. The next time he looked back, he was smiling. Could this be the first time in his life he'd run faster than one of his peers?

When Ernie finished the run, I was a good 15 seconds behind him—barely ahead of the next two runners. When I got to the finish, Ernie was positively beaming in excitement. My ankle was throbbing.

"Way to go, Willie," he puffed, patting me on the back. "You gave me a run for my money."

Felix was sitting on the grass catching his breath. "Ernie," Felix said. "Willie only lost because—"

I frowned and shook my head at Felix. He stopped in mid-sentence.

"Willie only lost because he was matched against *you*, Ernie," Felix said, though he was looking at me the whole time. "He probably would have beat *me* easily."

Ernie grinned. "I don't think I've ever run that fast," he said, shaking his head in disbelief.

When we'd all finished the mile run, Coach had us sit down while he tabulated our scores from the last few weeks. At the end of the period he read the names of all the kids who'd passed the Governor's Physical Fitness Exam. He called out every name but Big Ernie's and mine—I'd run the slowest mile of the entire class.

On the way to the locker room, Big Ernie put his arm over my shoulder. He was still beaming. "It's okay, Willie," he told me. "We'll get 'em next year."

I just smiled and shook my head. The tables had sure turned today: Little Ernie was now a school bully, and Big Ernie was consoling *me*!

Saturday was the final game of the Gophers' baseball season. We were up against the Hutchison Hawks, the district's first-place team. It was a must-win situation if we were going to get to our first play-offs. But no one seemed worried. We were on a roll now that Vincent Espinoza was back on top. Nothing could stop us now!

When I got to the field that day, it looked like the Fourth of July picnic in Central Park. The place was swarming with kids. Music was playing. Everyone seemed to be wearing the Gopher colors. Banners were flying everywhere. There was even one that said, "THANK YOU MYSTERY WRITER." It was hard to believe this was just a junior high school baseball game.

I walked around watching everyone have fun. No one knew it, but this was all because of me. If I hadn't given Vincent Espinoza that advice, none of us would be here. I might not have passed the Governor's Physical Fitness Exam, but I was still hot stuff.

Felix, Sam, Phoebe, and I could only get seats at the very top corner of the bleacher. This was nothing like the last game we'd been to!

The game was exhausting. The Gophers kept edging ahead, and then the Hawks would get back on top. But there was a gleam in the Gophers players' eyes. Even when we were behind, it *felt* like we were going to win. Coach Askew stood at the top of the dugout steps wringing his hands.

By the time we got to the ninth inning we were all hoarse from yelling. We were one run down with two outs, but the bases were loaded, and it was Vincent's turn at bat. This was his chance to send the Gophers to the playoffs in style!

When Vincent came to bat I had to cover my ears, the crowd was so loud. He came up to the plate look-

ing confident. He knocked the dirt out of his cleats
with the bat and stepped into the batter's box. He
looked relaxed and happy, like someone who *loved*
playing this game—like someone who had waited his
whole life to be in this situation.

While the pitcher found his grip on the ball, Vincent gazed out at the center field fence, just the way
I'd told him to. He smiled. Butterflies filled my stomach. This wasn't just *his* moment of glory; it was mine
as well. In a way I was part of the team. In a way all
this cheering was for me.

The pitcher wiped the sweat off his brow. He was
feeling the pressure. When the first pitch came, it
actually took a bounce before it got to the plate. The
catcher dove on it and covered it up so the runner on
third couldn't score. The pitcher just shook his head.
He was rattled.

The second pitch made it to the catcher without
bouncing, but it was high and outside. Ball two. Vincent was ahead in the count. Everything was going his
way. He smiled and backed out of the box a second.
He looked out at the fences again and took a deep,
relaxed breath. When he got back in his stance, he
was practically grinning.

The third pitch was a curve ball, but Vincent got
his bat on it, and it spun out over the left bleachers
into foul territory. The umpire gave the catcher a new
ball. While the pitcher rubbed it with his hands, Vincent gazed above his head to the center field fences.

From my higher perspective I could see a girl with long black hair on the lawn behind the fence. Some enterprising girl was out there waiting for the home run that would finally get the Gophers to the playoffs. I wished I'd thought of that.

The fourth pitch was so high, the catcher had to jump up and catch it like an outfielder backed against the fence. Ball three and only one strike. In a way it would be disappointing; if Vincent got walked, it would rob him of his chance to hit a grand slam.

The next pitch was a fat fast ball right down the middle. Vincent swung hard and connected. The ball sailed up and along the third base line. It was definitely going to clear the fence. Everyone on the bleachers stood and cheered, but when the ball left the field, it was just a shade to the left of the vertical line painted on the fence. The umpire called it foul. Strike two.

I expected the girl out beyond the fences to run and get the ball, but she ignored it. She was fiddling with something but I couldn't see what it was. I leaned forward and squinted. It was Kajyo Yamamoto, the shy girl in my science class. What was *she* doing out there?

The count was full now. My stomach clenched. Everything depended on the next pitch. Coach Askew had taken off his cap and was twisting it in his hands. I glanced over at Felix. He was biting his lower lip. You could feel the tension in the air, but when Vincent stepped back in the box he was still smiling—he was actually enjoying himself. He was probably the only person there who remembered that this was just a game.

The pitcher glanced around himself at the runners on the bases. He looked pale. He knew he'd have to throw a strike. He looked like he'd rather be anywhere than on the mound right now.

Vincent got into his stance while the pitcher waited for the catcher's signal. Vincent gazed out at the center field fence again, closely following my advice. I looked for that smile to come over his face again, but instead this time his mouth dropped open.

I glanced out at center field. Kajyo Yamamoto was hanging over the fence unfurling a giant banner.

"What is she *doing* out there?" Felix said beside me.

The banner was completely unfurled now. I leaned forward and squinted again.

I got that falling sensation again. I didn't have the nerve to tell Felix, but I knew *exactly* what she was doing. Vincent Espinoza was the boy she liked—the boy who didn't know she was alive. *You need to think*

of some dramatic way to get his attention, I'd told her in my column. *The more dramatic it is, the more likely you are to get (and keep) his attention.* I groaned and slapped my forehead. Another Glenfield student takes Amy's advice!

Vincent was still standing there with his mouth open when the pitcher went into his windup. The pitch was a fast ball right down the middle. It had home run written all over it. But Vincent didn't even see it. I don't think he even heard it slap the catcher's glove. He just stood there looking out at center field with a puzzled look on his face. The bleachers fell suddenly silent. The game was over, and Vincent didn't even know it.

"That was odd," Phoebe said.

"Shut up, Phoebe," I told her.

The Glenfield bleachers began to empty out. Everyone shuffled dejectedly toward the parking lot. I looked around at all the sad faces; only Felix looked excited.

"What's the matter with you?" I asked him. "We just lost the game, and you look happy about it."

"I'm not happy we lost," he said. "I'm happy I got the scoop."

"What scoop?"

"Mysterious Writer Dashes Glenfield Hopes," he said. "I'm going to interview Vincent and Kajyo." Felix headed over to the Glenfield dugout.

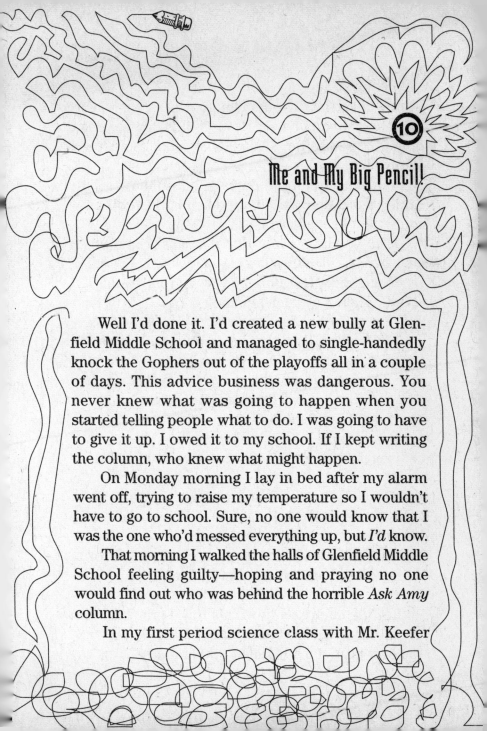

10

Me and My Big Pencil!

Well I'd done it. I'd created a new bully at Glen-field Middle School and managed to single-handedly knock the Gophers out of the playoffs all in a couple of days. This advice business was dangerous. You never knew what was going to happen when you started telling people what to do. I was going to have to give it up. I owed it to my school. If I kept writing the column, who knew what might happen.

On Monday morning I lay in bed after my alarm went off, trying to raise my temperature so I wouldn't have to go to school. Sure, no one would know that I was the one who'd messed everything up, but *I'd* know.

That morning I walked the halls of Glenfield Middle School feeling guilty—hoping and praying no one would find out who was behind the horrible *Ask Amy* column.

In my first period science class with Mr. Keefer

no one talked to Kajyo Yamamoto. She sat there more
quiet and shy than ever. How would she ever come
out of her shell after what had happened? And it was
all my fault.

Add that to all the damage I'd done by telling
Ernie Pignatello to stand up to Leonard Grubb. How
could things get any worse?

"Did you hear about Boris Dragas?" Sam asked
me when she sat down next to me in the cafeteria.

I laughed. "Did Phoebe put you up to this?" I
asked. "There's no such person."

"Yes, there is," Sam told me.

"Yeah, right," I said. "Who's going to give their kid
a name like that? Nobody's *really* called Boris—
except for the bad guy on *Rocky and Bullwinkle*."

"*Some* people call their kids Boris," Sam said.

"Yeah?" I said. "Like who?"

"Like people in Croatia."

I laughed again. "What's *that* have to do with anything?"

"Because Boris is from Croatia," Sam said. "He's
an exchange student. He got here a few weeks ago.
And now he's in the hospital."

Sam didn't look like she was kidding, and for a
few seconds I almost fell for it. "Nah," I told her.
"Phoebe put you up to this."

Just then Felix set down his tray. I grinned. This
was my chance to call Sam's bluff. "Hey, Felix," I said.
"You ever hear of a guy called Boris Dragas?"

"The exchange student?" he said. "Yeah. He sits across from me in social studies—but he wasn't in class this morning."

I got that falling feeling yet again—I was headed for the basement on the express elevator.

"He's in the hospital," Sam said to Felix. "He had some kind of nasty fall. He broke some bones, but they think he'll be OK."

"Poor guy," Felix said. "He's barely off the plane and something like this happens."

I thought about the letter—the recent plane trip, the plane trip yet to come. No wonder he misspelled *heights*; English was his second language!

"What's the matter, Willie?" Sam asked. "You don't look so good."

"It was him," I croaked.

"What was who?" Felix asked.

"The kid with the fear of heights," I said. "The one I told to go climb a cliff. The one who wrote a letter to Amy."

Sam's mouth dropped open. "You said that was a *joke*," Sam said. "You said *Phoebe* wrote that letter."

"That's what I thought," I said. "I thought Boris was the little man in her sock drawer. I thought she was setting me up for something."

"So you sent Glenfield's only exchange student to the quarry to climb a cliff?" Sam sputtered. "Do you realize what you've done?"

"Dude," Felix said. "This is an international inci-
dent. There could be a war." He seemed oddly excited
by the prospect. "Where *is* Croatia? I bet we can take
them."

"There's *not* going to be a war," Sam said. "But it
sure isn't going to make Glenfield look good if this
story gets out."

"MYSTERY WRITER MAIMS FOREIGN VISI-
TOR," Felix said. "Hey, that's pretty good!" He took
the top off his hamburger and asked Sam to pass the
ketchup.

I groaned. "This could only happen to me," I said.
I put my forehead on the edge of the table and closed
my eyes.

I still had my head on the cool table top when I
heard a high-pitched voice growl, "Gimmie that, Four-
Eyes."

I lifted my head to see Ernie Pignatello snatch the
squeeze bottle of ketchup out of Felix's hand. He
sneered and gave Felix a shove. "*Geek*," he said and
walked away with the ketchup.

Felix watched him walk away. "You know I liked
him a lot more *before* you started giving him advice,"
Felix told me.

That night my stomach was twisted so tight, I
barely touched my dinner. Afterwards I just went
upstairs and lay on my bed without turning on the
light. I was miserable.

As I lay there, staring up at the dark ceiling, it occurred to me that maybe Felix and Sam were *both* pulling my leg. Phoebe was much better at pulling practical jokes than I'd given her credit for. Maybe she *had* set the whole thing up.

The more I thought about it, the better I felt. How could I have been such a sap? Of *course* it was a joke! If there *was* a Boris Dragas in school, I'd never heard of him. It had to be a prank. But if I wanted to know for sure, I'd have to talk to someone who couldn't possibly be in on the joke.

I went down to the kitchen and found the phone book. I looked up the number I needed. I dialed.

"Glenfield Medical Center," an older woman's voice answered.

"Yes," I said. "I heard that an acquaintance of mine is in the hospital. Could you tell me his room number?"

"Certainly," she said. "What is his name?"

"Boris Dragas," I told her. I heard the sound of computer keys clicking. I waited.

"I don't find any listing here for a Boris Dragas," the woman said.

I grinned. It felt like the weight of the world had been lifted from my shoulders. It *was* all a joke!

"Wait a minute," the voice on the phone said. "*Here* it is. He's in room 318."

"He's what?" I croaked.

"He's in room 318," the voice said. "Would you like me to put you through?"

"No, thank you," I managed to say.

It took me several tries to get the phone back on its cradle.

All day Tuesday I wandered through school in a daze. I even got yelled at by little Ernie Pignatello for brushing up against him in the hall.

At lunch Felix showed me his next feature article: Mysterious Writer Linked To Exchange Student Injury. It included a hospital room interview with Boris and a detailed description of his many injuries.

"You can't print this," I said.

"Why not?" he asked.

"Because you're my friend," I said. "Everyone's going to kill me when they find out who's been writing *Ask Amy*."

"This isn't personal," Felix said. "I've *got* to write this. It's is a scoop, and I'm a journalist."

"You're going to be scooping up your own teeth if this gets in the paper," I threatened. I was *that* angry.

"OK, OK," he said. "Chill out, Willie. I'll write about something else."

That night Sam called me on the phone.

"Felix and I are going to the hospital tomorrow after school," she said. "We're going to go visit Boris. You think you might want to come with us?"

I held the phone to my ear a moment and didn't say anything. I was thinking. The last thing I wanted to do was face Boris, but I knew I should apologize to him and that I should do it in person. "Yeah," I said. "I'll go with you."

When I hung up the phone, I went upstairs to my room and lay down on the bed. This had all gone far enough. It was time for me to end it. I stared at the ceiling and thought about Vincent and Kajyo. I thought about how I'd encouraged Ernie to get into a fight with Leonard. I thought about how I'd sent Boris Dragas out to the quarry with a nylon rope. I was through giving advice.

I got up and went over to my desk. I turned on my desk lamp and got out a sheet of paper. I started writing my last *Ask Amy* column.

When I got to Miss Pell's classroom the next day after PE, her classroom door was locked, so I wrote a note on the back of my column:

Dear Miss Pell,

I'm sorry, but I will no longer be able to write the Ask Amy column for the school paper. Please print this letter instead of my usual column this week. Thank you for your patience and encouragement.

Wilbur Plummet

I slipped it under the door and headed for the flagpole. I was meeting Sam and Felix there, so the three of us could go visit Boris Dragas.

In the lobby of the hospital I stopped by the gift shop and bought some balloons and chocolates for Boris—at least his jaw wasn't wired shut. Felix led the way, since he'd actually been to the room before. The three of us got on the elevator and when the doors closed, Sam pressed the button for the third floor.

Hospitals always make me nervous—there's that smell and all that white light—but I don't think I'd ever been *this* nervous. I trudged down the long third floor corridor looking down at the gleaming floor tiles. In my mind I tried to think of what I could possibly say to Boris that would explain what I'd done to him.

When we got to the doorway of room 318, I looked inside. There was just one bed in the room. Someone was in the bed, but the covers were pulled up over the face.

"Oh, oh," Felix said ushering me and Sam into the room. "They've pulled the sheet over his face. Do you know what that means?"

I stood at the foot of the bed with my mouth hanging open. It felt like the floor had fallen out from under me. It was the worst thing that had ever happened to me. I'd actually **killed** Glenfield's first exchange student! I put my hand over my chest. I thought I felt a heart attack coming on.

"You *do* know what it means don't you?" Felix asked. He had an odd smile on his face, but I was so shocked, it didn't really register.

"It means that you're the world's biggest sap," a voice said from under the covers. Suddenly the body in the bed sat up. The sheet fell off. Phoebe sat there grinning up at me.

"What!?"

"I said, 'You're the world's biggest sap,' " Phoebe told me again. "You didn't really think there was a Boris Dragas, did you?"

"But how?" I sputtered.

"I got Felix and Sam to help me."

"Yeah," I said, "but I *called* the hospital. They said Boris was here."

Phoebe grinned. "Dr. Griffith," she explained. "It was such a mean trick you played on me by sending me to her house, she was happy to help. She put Boris' name in the hospital computer in case you checked."

I was shocked and relieved and angry and amused all at once. I had to admit this was probably the most elaborate practical joke in Glenfield history. My mind was still reeling. I had to sit down.

"OK," I said, plopping down on the edge of Phoebe's hospital bed. "You beat me. I surrender. This

practical joke war is over. You are the undisputed
Queen of Pranks in this town."

"Long live the Queen!" Felix said with a fake
British accent.

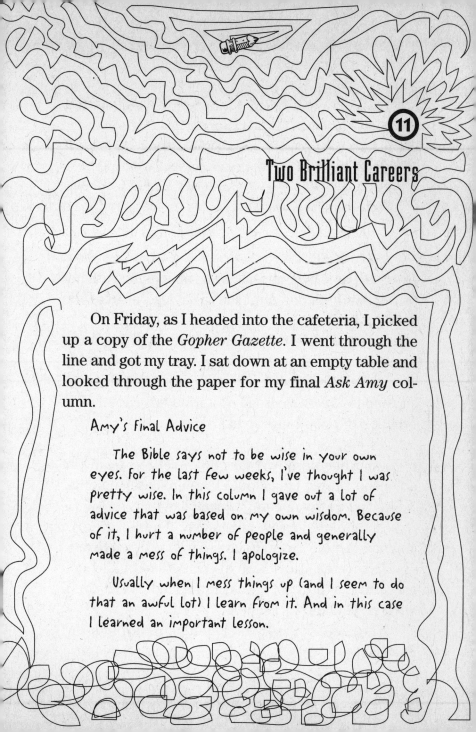

11

Two Brilliant Careers

On Friday, as I headed into the cafeteria, I picked up a copy of the *Gopher Gazette*. I went through the line and got my tray. I sat down at an empty table and looked through the paper for my final *Ask Amy* column.

Amy's Final Advice

The Bible says not to be wise in your own eyes. For the last few weeks, I've thought I was pretty wise. In this column I gave out a lot of advice that was based on my own wisdom. Because of it, I hurt a number of people and generally made a mess of things. I apologize.

Usually when I mess things up (and I seem to do that an awful lot) I learn from it. And in this case I learned an important lesson.

So here is my final advice to all of you: Human wisdom is imperfect and limited. So, when you've got a problem and you need the answer, there's a place you should go first before you write a letter to the school newspaper. God's wisdom is perfect. Seek His advice first.

And that's the last you'll hear from this mystery writer.

Sam came over and sat down next to me with her tray. "I saw your column," she said. "Are you sure you want to quit?"

"Are you kidding?" I said. "Give me a few more weeks, and I might *actually* start a war with Croatia."

Sam smiled. "Look on the bright side," she said. "It sounds like you learned a lot from this experience. I think it did you some good."

"I'll say."

"And maybe now that you're retired from the advice business, you should take up matchmaking."

"What do you mean?" I asked her.

Sam pointed a few tables over. There sat Kajyo Yamamoto and Vincent Espinoza having lunch together. They were sitting close to each other, talking quietly and laughing. My mouth dropped open. "Well, what do you know," I said.

"Hey, here comes Felix Patterson, star reporter," Sam said.

Felix sat down across from me. He was pretending to be glum. "I can't believe you're quitting on me."

"Are you serious?" I said. "Do you realize all the trouble I caused?"

"Yeah," he said. "That's what I mean. How can you do this to me?"

"What are you *talking* about?" I asked.

"If you quit, my career as a reporter is over too," Felix sniffed. "You were crucial to my career as a journalist."

I felt flattered. "Really?" I said. "I didn't think I gave you that much feedback."

"Feedback schmeedback," Felix said. "My plan was to follow you around and report on all the disasters you caused. I would have won a Pulitzer."

Sam spread her hands out in front of her. "Two Brilliant Journalism Careers End," she said, like she was reading the headline. "Middle School Barely Survives."

I couldn't keep from laughing. It was pretty close to the truth.